POWDER ISLAND

The series page at Amazon:
amzn.to/2s9U2jW

THE **SHERLOCK HOLMES/ LUCY JAMES** MYSTERIES

POWDER ISLAND

BY **ANNA ELLIOTT** AND **CHARLES VELEY**

This is a work of fiction. Names, characters, organizations, places, events, and incidents are either products of the author's imagination or are used fictitiously.

Typesetting by FormattingExperts.com
Cover design by Todd A. Johnson

ISBN: 978-0-9991191-9-8

1. WATSON

"Holmes," I said, putting aside my copy of the morning *Times*, "there was a massive explosion at Powder Island yesterday."

It was an April Monday, just after breakfast. The two of us were in our sitting-room, appreciating the warmth from the glowing coals in our fireplace. A cold rain lashed at our bow window.

"A man has died. Our old friend Gregson is involved. The report hints at murder."

Holmes leaned back in his armchair, fingers steepled and eyes closed. "Kindly be so good as to read the account."

This was the passage I read:

HORRIFIC EXPLOSION CLAIMS LIFE
AT POWDER ISLAND

At a few minutes before 9 o'clock Sunday morning, an enormous explosion shocked thousands of British citizens. The blast came from the Rexford Gunpowder Factory on the banks of the Thames at Hounslow. In the factory rubble, police found the skull and several fragments of a human body, assumed to be the remains of Mr. Marcus Thiel, 60 years old. Mr. Thiel had been the company supervisor of operations. He leaves behind a widow and daughter. By all accounts, Mr. Thiel had been employed by the firm for many years and had been meticulous in the performance of his duties.

Authorities do not believe the explosion was due to carelessness. Inspector Tobias Gregson of the Metropolitan Police will lead an investigation into the cause of the tragedy.

Nearly four hundred workers at the factory have been suspended, including about 70 women. Until the investigation and rebuilding operations are complete, nearly all will remain unemployed.

I put down the newspaper. My heart felt heavy as I thought of the man's violent death, and of the four hundred employees without work, and their need for justice. I turned to Holmes. "'Not due to carelessness,'" I repeated. "That suggests a more sinister force behind the explosion, does it not?"

Holmes nodded. "I shall await a call from Inspector Gregson," he said. "It would be good to work with him again."

But springtime passed, and then summer, and then autumn, and finally winter began, and the call from Inspector Gregson did not come.

2. LUCY

The shrill ring of the telephone yanked me out of sleep.

I opened my eyes and frowned, slowly coming alert. Snowflakes were falling outside our window. Jack's side of the bed was empty, and the telephone's ringing had stopped. Which meant that early as it was, Jack was already awake and had gone to answer it.

I got up, slipping on my dressing gown and heading for the stairs to follow him. I walked on tiptoe, on the chance that Becky was miraculously still asleep. I could hear Jack's voice coming from the front hall below.

"I want you to check every square inch of his rooms."

He had to be speaking to one of the police constables under his command. He was using what I thought of as his sergeant's voice: crisp and firm with authority. Although I thought this morning there was a more than usual grimness to his tone.

"Look behind the furniture, take up the carpets, send someone to sweep the chimney and unscrew the light fixtures if you have to. Understood, Hutchins?"

Constable Hutchins must have replied in the affirmative, because Jack hung up the telephone's speaking piece.

I would have sworn I hadn't made any noise, but he hadn't spent two years walking a beat in some of London's most dangerous neighbourhoods without developing a sixth sense as to whether or not he was alone.

He turned his head to look at me. "Good morning. Sorry if I woke you."

"It's all right." I tightened the belt of my robe and came the rest of the way down the stairs. "I was just waiting for you to add that if mathematicians can prove the existence of a fourth dimension, Constable Hutchins should search there, too."

Jack smiled, though briefly.

He was already dressed, his shirtsleeves rolled up and his dark hair rumpled as though he'd been running his hands through it.

I looked past him to our front room, where stacks of paper covered the table.

"Are those the reports on Sergeant O'Hara's murder?"

A little less than a week ago O'Hara had been killed. Jack had known him since the early days of their careers on the police force. Jack's unit at Scotland Yard had been assigned to the case.

Jack followed my glance. "That's right. Just going over witness reports."

"Witnesses?" O'Hara had been found in a dirty back alley in Whitechapel with a knife between his shoulder blades. I hadn't heard there were any witnesses.

"Witnesses might be too strong a word." Jack picked up one of the sheets of paper. "Just statements from people in the area. A couple of beggars who were parked in a doorway not far off at the time. A troupe of street performers—clowns." Jack raised an eyebrow. "I can't wait to hear what Hutchins has to say after interviewing them."

Unlike the cases Watson wrote about, which were generally solved with a single stroke of Holmes's brilliance, most police work was accomplished with hours upon hours of painful interviews and then combing through many possibly inaccurate, often contradictory reports, searching for the smallest details that might provide a fresh piece of the puzzle.

Jack picked up another paper, frowning. "Then there's a couple of sailors on shore leave who were going back to their ship after a night in the grog shops and heard shouts coming from the alley where O'Hara was found—or somewhere close by. They didn't think anything of it till they saw the story in the newspaper and came in to the Yard to make a report."

"Do you think they may actually have heard the murder?"

"I doubt it. Hearing shouts in Whitechapel is about as rare as a foggy day. And stabbing someone in the back implies stealth—you don't put your victim on his guard by shouting at him from behind."

Jack's voice was perfectly level, but the line of his mouth had tightened, and his eyes were dark with a cold, distant look that made a shiver slide through me.

He looked like a man who'd been fully expecting the worst and had just been proven right.

I opened my mouth, then closed it again.

None of this explained why Jack was so insistent that Sergeant O'Hara's room be searched. But—

Jack looked up at me. "You're about to ask why this case in particular bothers me."

"I didn't say a single thing!"

He smiled, if faintly. "Yeah, if you'd said nothing any louder, I'd be deaf right about now." He sighed. "It's not that I don't want to tell you—"

"It's all right. You don't have to, I understand."

There were always aspects of official police cases that Jack wasn't at liberty to share with me. It wouldn't be fair to try to make him tell me more than his duties allowed.

Jack shook his head. "No, I—"

Beside me, the telephone rang, making me startle. I reached for the receiver. "I'll answer. But it's probably Constable Hutchins again."

When I picked up, though, the voice I heard on the other end of the line belonged to my father, Sherlock Holmes.

"Ah, Lucy." As usual, Holmes forbore to waste time on anything as conventional as words of greeting. "I'm glad you are already awake. I have a question for Jack, if he is available?"

I felt my eyebrows edge upwards. It was seldom that Holmes needed to consult the police for answers, even his own son-in-law. "Yes, he's here."

Jack came to stand next to me, and I held the earpiece out so we both could listen.

"Good." Holmes's voice came crackling through the telephone line. "I need your recollections of the explosion at Powder Island."

3. LUCY

Jack's expression registered surprise—as I was sure did mine.

"Powder Island?" he repeated with a grimace. "Not my favourite case."

"You worked it with Gregson, as I recall," Holmes said on the other end of the telephone line.

"I did. Nine months ago. Gregson was convinced it was arson and homicide, and so was I. He got into a good deal of trouble over it, poor bloke."

"How?"

"He trusted his superiors."

"Who, specifically?"

Jack looked uncomfortable. "I don't know, specifically. But someone high up didn't want him going on with that case. He persisted, and when he wouldn't back away, he lost his rank. Now he's been broken down to a beat copper, and he's walking the streets and alleys of Whitechapel."

"Can you get me the file?" Holmes asked.

Jack nodded, but his brows were furrowed. "How soon do you need it?"

"The factory owner wants to meet with me at eleven o'clock this morning."

"In that case, I'll go in to the Yard straight away."

"I'll come with you," I said. "You can give the files to me and I'll bring them on to Baker Street."

* * *

Snow was falling thickly as Jack and I made our way along the embankment towards Scotland Yard. Becky dashed ahead of us, the ends of her red scarf flapping as she tried to catch the flakes on her tongue.

She looked so joyful, even the surliest-looking passers-by didn't object when she narrowly missed bumping into them.

"That would be good news for Inspector Gregson," I said, "if his theory of foul play at the gunpowder factory could be proven correct."

"Hmm." Jack's eyes were on the Thames beside us, busy even in the wintry weather with steam launches and river barges, but I doubted he was seeing them. His voice and his gaze were both abstracted.

I looked up at him sharply. Jack was *never* abstracted—especially not when he was out on the streets with both me and Becky. He, like most police officers who'd seen far too much of the city's most violent side, constantly scanned his surroundings, noting details, evaluating potential threats. The habit was so ingrained in him as to be automatic by now.

"Maybe chimpanzees escaped from the Hyde Park zoo," I said. "They might have swum across the river, and let off fireworks to ignite an explosion."

"Could be."

"Jack!"

Jack started and looked down at me, then rubbed the space between his eyes. "Sorry. I was just thinking about—" he shook his head. "Never mind. What were you saying?"

"I was asking about the Powder Island case. Why couldn't Gregson prove it was actually arson?"

"We never really got that far. We collected the evidence, took witness statements—and then word came down from the assistant commissioner. The case was to be handed over to the Home Office. Gregson argued against it. Didn't want to give the investigation up. That's what lost him his rank. The Home Office men took offense—thought he should have given them better cooperation. Next thing I heard, he was broken down to constable."

"Was that the only reason? Just because he didn't cooperate with the Home Office?"

"How do you mean?"

"I don't know. But it feels as though there must be something wrong—or at the very least odd—about the case."

Particularly since Holmes was now involved. My father didn't undertake investigations unless either the stakes were especially high or the problem was an especially knotty one.

In the case of an explosion at a gunpowder factory, both of those conditions might well be proven true.

We had reached Scotland Yard. Becky came darting back to tug at my hand. "Lucy, can we go around to the stables and see the horses? Please?"

"All right." The Scotland Yard official horses were kept in a stable area in an inner courtyard of the building. "Jack can go and fetch the file and then meet us out there?" I glanced questioningly at Jack.

"That's fine." Jack paused, though, with his foot on the first step leading up to the Yard's entrance. He looked back at me with a puzzled frown. "Did you say something about chimpanzees?"

Jack looked grim enough, though, when he came outside and found us a quarter of an hour later.

Becky was delightedly feeding extra measures of oats to the horses and laughing when their velvet lips tickled the palm of her hand.

"What is it?" I asked.

"The files on Powder Island are missing."

"Missing?"

Jack took out a slip of paper and held it out. "This is all that's left."

The paper was a transfer slip, indicating the files had been signed over to the Home Office.

Jack nodded. "Everything else—all the notes and the statements taken from the witnesses—is gone."

I looked up at him, hesitating.

Jack sighed. "All right. I'll write a note to him."

"How do you know what I was about to ask?"

"Detective, remember?" Jack tapped his forehead. "Just be careful. Those aren't good neighborhoods to be walking around in."

"I will be."

Becky came back to join us, looking from me to Jack. "What's happened? Is something wrong?"

"Not yet. But after we visit Baker Street to tell Holmes about the missing file, we're going to make a visit to Whitechapel to track down Police Constable Gregson."

4. WATSON

A cab, an ordinary growler, cut across the snowy traffic lanes on Baker Street, heading straight for our home. I was close by on the pavement, returning from a morning errand, my boots growing steadily more soaked from the slush.

The cab was drawn by a single horse and driven by an ordinary cabman. The fellow wore a red wool scarf. He hunched over his reins. As soon as he reached the curb, he pulled his horse to a stop, directly in front of 221B and only a few feet ahead of where I stood.

The driver made no move to dismount. I saw no sign of activity within the enclosed carriage.

Perhaps, I thought, Holmes was about to dash off to some adventure without me. Using my own key, I quickly let myself in to our downstairs hallway and mounted the seventeen steps more briskly than usual.

But upon opening the door to our sitting room, it was plain that Holmes was very much at home and not at all about to depart. The papers from the past week lay in an untidy heap beside his desk, and Holmes himself lounged in his customary chair beside a blazing fire, pipe in hand, his sharp features enveloped in clouds of blue-grey tobacco smoke.

He glanced first at me and then at his watch.

"You ran up the steps," Holmes said. "Is he here?"

"You are expecting a client?"

"At eleven."

"There was a cab," I said. "I thought it was empty."

Holmes stood as I hung up my coat, and together we went to our bow window.

"Which cab?" Holmes asked.

For now, there were two cabs. The one I had noticed, with the forlorn-looking driver in his red scarf, had not moved. Behind it, however, another growler had stopped. Its driver had dismounted from his perch and was opening the door for a passenger.

"The first."

"The other has brought our client," Holmes said, "that tall, bearded fellow getting out now. Bradley Rexford is his name."

Rexford descended from the growler swathed in a black fur coat. Ignoring the cabby's proffered arm, he clapped a top hat onto his balding head, stuffed a folded note into the cabby's hand with a swift, final gesture, and then strode past, holding a black leather briefcase and mounting the steps to our front stoop. We heard the ring of our bell-pull.

Holmes grasped the window shade and pulled it down. Then he raised it once more, slowly.

I saw Flynn across the street, in the doorway of a coffee shop where he had been warming himself. Alerted by Holmes's signal with the window shade, he was looking at us.

"Why Flynn?" I asked.

"The first cab," Holmes said.

The cab driven by the man in the red scarf had not moved. But from here, I could see through the small viewing panel cut into the rear. A shadowy presence indicated a passenger was inside.

"Away from the window, if you please, old friend," Holmes said. "When our client arrives, I shall excuse myself. At that time, be so good as to entertain Mr. Rexford for a moment or two."

"You'll be giving instructions to Flynn," I was about to say, but the heavy footsteps on our stairs were nearly at our door and Holmes was pressing a finger to his lips for silence.

* * *

"Where is he going?" Rexford turned his square-cut face to me as the door closed behind Holmes. A greying beard fringed his jawline and chin, and it quivered with indignation.

"He won't be long," I replied. "Please. Do have a seat."

Rexford set down his briefcase and carefully draped his heavy, glossy coat over the back of our settee. Powerfully built, though somewhat stooped in age, he stood for a few moments to survey the room, his arms akimbo, reminding me of the great statue of King Henry VIII above the gateway at Saint Bart's hospital, in his characteristic pose of dominion and defiance.

I determined to be polite. "May I offer you a cigarette? A cigar?"

"I never smoke. Too great a hazard in my business."

"Which is?"

His lips pressed together for a moment. "I take it Mr. Holmes has not told you. I own the Rexford Works on Powder Island. Largest gunpowder manufacturer in Europe."

I recalled the newspaper article. "Where a significant explosion occurred last year," I said.

The pride in his expression turned to discomfort. "My appointment was for eleven. It is now—" he stopped, reaching into his waistcoat pocket. Then, abruptly, he withdrew his hand. "I had forgotten. Misplaced my watch somehow." He quickly added, "It's a damn fine watch, but that's not what brings me here."

He sat down heavily on our settee. "And I won't want you writing about it," he said.

"You may rest assured," I said.

A moment later, to my relief, I heard Holmes's footsteps on our stairs.

"Just one more moment," Holmes said as he entered. He strode swiftly to our bow window and looked out. He watched intently, holding up his hand for silence.

Then he turned. "My apologies for the delay, Mr. Rexford. How can I be of assistance?"

In answer, Rexford withdrew a sheaf of papers from his briefcase and held them out to Holmes. "I want you to read this first."

Holmes took the papers without glancing at them. "Is that the Home Office report on the explosion at your factory?"

Rexford said, "I am impressed."

Now seated in his familiar chair by the fireside, Holmes crossed his legs, leaned back and steepled his fingertips. "Then please state your business."

"First, I wish you to clear up the uncertainty created by the report."

Holmes nodded. "Understandably." He nodded to me. "Watson, you may wish to refer to this—" he waved at the pages with a dismissive gesture. "Mycroft provided me a copy yesterday. It runs on for dozens of pages, close-set in type at the public's expense by Her Majesty's Inspector of Explosives, prepared for the Home Office. I shall summarise, in the interest of your time, Mr. Rexford, the thousands and thousands of words in the report and its exhibits. Pray correct me if I misstate."

Rexford nodded.

"There was an explosion some nine months ago in the glazing house of your gunpowder works. The blast was heard for miles and it demolished the building entirely. The scattered remains of only one man were found. The unfortunate victim was the supervisor of the works, known to be a reliable, conscientious and experienced man. At nine o'clock in the morning he was the only man scheduled to be on duty, for the day was a Sunday and work had halted for the Sabbath. The report lists ten possible causes of the explosion and dismisses eight of those ten, leaving as possibilities only the breakdown of a mechanical part of the mixing-equipment, which would have produced friction and thus a spark, or a flame from the heads of lucifer matches, which might have been scattered on the platform by a person or persons unknown for malicious purposes."

"Matches had been found on the floor in one of the other buildings," added Rexford. "A few days earlier."

"So now you come to me," said Holmes. "After nine months and a police inspection and a Home Office report, all with no results, you come to me. After the trail has gone cold, and after police have questioned all the witnesses. And you must know that I have no authority to require more answers."

"I had hoped the report—"

Homes held up his hand. "Pardon my interruption, Mr. Rexford. But you mistake my meaning. I did not ask why you waited to come, but why you come to me at all."

Rexford took a plain white envelope from his inside pocket

and handed it to Holmes. "Because yesterday morning I received this."

The envelope contained a single sheet of cheap paper, on which had been pasted words clipped from a newspaper. The words of the message read:

Don't be too quick to celebrate. Another big bang is coming your way.

5. FLYNN

Flynn's icy fingers were slipping. It was awkward enough keeping his face away from the little window at the back of the slow-moving cab. Each time the wheels bumped over the ruts in the frozen slush, he lost just a little of his grip on the rooftop. He knew he would fall, unless he could somehow rebalance himself. Wiry, nearly twelve, Flynn was pretty sure he could do that.

Twisting his torso towards the back corner, he heaved himself upwards, scrabbling for the now-empty iron rail that would have kept suitcases from sliding off the roof, if there had been any suitcases. The fingertips of his right hand got around it. Numb though they were, they hooked the luggage rail like claws.

He was swinging his body back so as to get his other hand on the rail, when the cab stopped.

The side door clicked open.

Flynn bent to peer into the cab through the rear viewing pane. He saw a shadowy black-caped figure, and a gloved hand gripping the strap of a grey canvas holdall bag. Then the figure and the canvas bag were out the door. The cab lurched forwards just as Flynn dropped to the slush-crusted roadway. Off balance, Flynn fell into the slush, soaking the knees of his trousers. Thankfully, his boots kept the wet away from his feet and they gave him good traction as he stood. Mr. Mycroft had given him the boots, sturdy leather with strong leather laces, as a present for his work identifying some bombers just before Christmas.

Flynn took no thought of that past success, though he was grateful for the boots. At the moment he knew he was on the verge of failing in the assignment Mr. Holmes had given him, first to watch the entrance to 221B Baker Street in anticipation of an important client this morning, and then to follow the cab driven by the man in the red scarf and not to lose sight of the passenger.

Out of the way, y' nickey dimwit!

A lorry driver was yelling that he was an idiot. The two big dray lorry horses were about to trample him. He'd be a dead idiot, he thought, if he didn't get a move on.

But across the street on the pavement, a black-caped figure in a white captain's cap was striding away from him, with a grey canvas holdall bag swinging alongside. The man was heading towards the round arches of the nearest building.

Flynn took that direction, scrambled after the caped figure, a hoof of the lead horse connecting with his retreating boot. The smack stung his ankle and knocked him off balance, but he kept on. He could read the sign above the arch. This was the entrance to the Baker Street Station of the Metropolitan Line.

He could buy a ticket, he told himself. He had a half-crown in his pocket. He would just see which train the caped figure boarded, wait to be sure the figure stayed on the train, and then climb onto the last car at the last minute.

A crowd was coming up the stairs, soot-covered and hurrying to reach the fresher outdoor air. As they surged round Flynn, he lost sight of the caped figure and the captain's cap.

Heart pounding, he pushed his way down the stairs. He waited a few steps above the platform, surveying the people waiting to board.

No white captain's cap.

No black cape.

No grey canvas holdall bag.

Flynn turned and scrambled back up the stairs. He hustled away from the entry doors, into the upper part of the station, where passengers could buy their tickets and get bread and coffee and meat pies and such. He made a quick circuit of the area.

No white captain's cap. No black cape. No grey bag.

Failure. He would have to go back to Baker Street at once and tell Mr. Holmes.

6. WATSON

"What is the celebration to which this note refers?" Holmes said.

"Our factory is almost ready to resume full operation," Rexford said. "A dinner is being planned tomorrow at the local church." His expression softened, and his voice took on a note of appeal. "I am getting on in years, Mr. Holmes. The responsibility for the lives of others is a burden that grows heavier as one ages. I am only a man, after all. I beg you, do not mention this threat to anyone in the course of your investigation."

"You ought not to assume that I have accepted your case, Mr. Rexford."

"I shall pay five hundred pounds—"

"My fees are not in question."

"Five thousand—"

"Not unless I can determine that it would be worth your money and my time."

"There are many whose livelihoods depend on it. Four hundred employees and their families."

"And when the explosion occurred last April, all of them had been quite content with their positions and wages?"

Rexford stroked his chin. "I wouldn't say all. Not so rosy as that. We had our share of complaints. Some talk of forming a trade union. Not that our operation can sustain a pay raise—the government is our major customer, and they're not about to give us more generous terms. Not when they can get product from our competitors."

"Who is the current supervisor of the works on Powder Island?"

"My son Rex now manages the operation. He did not wish to do so, knowing what had happened to his predecessor. But he has taken up the task regardless of the risk and has done very well, by all accounts. Very thorough and conscientious—"

"Thank you. Are any others of your family employed at the works?"

"I have no other children. And my wife died fifteen years ago."

"Any other relations, more distant ones, perhaps?"

"There is my niece. My sister's daughter. She is my personal clerk."

"She telephoned me yesterday morning to make this appointment. And is your sister still alive?"

"She is. But her husband is not."

Holmes raised one eyebrow inquiringly.

"He was the previous supervisor of the works."

"Killed in the explosion."

Rexford nodded. "A sad day. I ought to have told you at first."

Holmes made a dismissive gesture. "And who is the beneficiary of your estate?"

"My son inherits all. Other than a small annuity for my sister and a few other bequests."

"And would that hold true if you were to float the business on the public exchange, as you are planning to do?"

Rexford's eyes widened. "How do you know that? The arrangements for incorporation have been a closely guarded secret."

"The government has its ways of learning when the largest

supplier of a commodity essential to the security of the Empire is about to change ownership." Holmes paused. I immediately thought of Mycroft.

Rexford gave a great sigh. "Of course. And yes, my son's inheritance would be unchanged. But my son would inherit shares instead of direct ownership."

"He would attain wealth, without the burden of responsibility."

"I think it would be best for him. He is a fine, strong, adventurous lad—he reminds me of myself in my younger days. He has done well enough managing the operation these past nine months. However, he is still young."

"He does not know of your plans?"

Rexford's voice trembled. "No, Mr. Holmes, he does not! And I beg you, do not tell him."

"Why not?"

"Because he would think I had doubts as to his competence for the supervisory position. And concerns for his safety."

"But you do have such doubts and concerns, do you not?"

"Any father would. I shall be most relieved when an impartial new management selects a third-party supervisor. The death of my brother-in-law was a severe emotional blow."

"Where were you when the blast occurred?"

"In church, across the river from the factory. It was a Sunday morning. I was there with Rex. My sister and my niece were there too. It was a shocking moment, I can tell you, Mr. Holmes. The blast shook the ground and rattled the very benches we knelt upon. My son and I ran across the bridge, and we saw the smoking ruins from up close."

"You were able to keep up with your son?"

Rexford shook his head. "As I said, I am getting older far

more rapidly than I would wish. I recall coming over the rise, and seeing his silhouette, bent over, slumped in dejection and shock. His hands were on his knees. Beyond him was utter desolation. The memory—well, it keeps me awake at night, Mr. Holmes."

"Understandable."

Rexford leaned forwards. "Now, Mr. Holmes, will you take the case?"

"One moment," Holmes said. He got to his feet, strode across to our bow window once again, adjusted the shade, and looked out.

7. FLYNN

"You, boy!"

Flynn heard a woman's voice behind him. She sounded breathless.

About to mount the steps of 221B Baker Street, Flynn turned. He saw a young woman crossing the street towards him, her dirty face tarted up with rouge and lip colour, her dark hair bedraggled beneath a ragged linen scarf, her wool coat and skirt looking as if she'd slept in them, and in an alley at that. The hem of her long skirt dragged in the slush.

She stood just at the edge of the curb. "Saw you talkin' wi' Mr. Holmes, right there in 'is doorway."

"What of it?"

"I saw you hop on the back of that cab and stick to it like a bug."

She was trying to smile and talk at the same time, but she kept her lips together. Probably she was ashamed of her teeth, Flynn thought. She was all tight and tense, her hands clasped in front of her like she was praying, only she was holding something. Flynn couldn't see what it was.

"So?"

"I figured you'd fall off and come back to tell 'im wot 'appened, so I waited. And here you are."

"Tell 'im what?"

"Never mind." She shook her head, and the scarf slipped to one side. She quickly straightened it, awkwardly, because she was still holding the something in both hands. "I want you to do sommat for me. I want you to give this to Mr. Holmes."

And she held out a gold pocket watch. Flynn took it.

"Where'd you get this?"

"Nicked it, didn't I? I want Mr. Holmes to give it back."

"Wot you want to do that for? Looks a ream flash jerry."

For a moment she seemed confused. Then she recovered. "Oh. Right. But 'e'll kill me and my friend if 'e don't get it back. 'E knows she took it, you see. Or 'e will know, soon enough. And 'e's a right dangerous man to cross."

"Where'd you nick it?"

"My friend nicked it, really. At the Blue Bottle. 'E goes there to see 'er reg'lar, and she knows 'e'll figure out she's the one who nicked it, because 'e's a big powerful rich smart bloke, and now she's dreadful scared of wot 'e'll do to 'er."

"What's his name?"

"'E don't say it at the Blue Bottle, but there's writin' on the watch. Should be easy enough for Mr. Holmes to figure it out. That's why my friend is so dreadful scared. That's why she can't return the watch herself. Because now the rich bloke will think she knows 'is name."

Flynn looked up to Mr. Holmes's bow window. He saw Mr. Holmes, gesturing at him, indicating he should wait.

8. WATSON

After nearly two minutes at our bow window, Holmes turned back to us and addressed Rexford. "I crave your patience, Mr. Rexford. I must leave you once again, but it will not be for long, and upon my return I may be able to provide you the answer you are seeking."

Before Rexford could protest, Holmes was gone.

9. FLYNN

Flynn saw Mr. Holmes leave the window.

Still holding the gold pocket watch, he turned back to ask more questions of the young woman. But she was running away, across Baker Street, one hand clapped on top of her scarf. Her boots splashed in the slush as she dodged a carriage. Then an omnibus blocked Flynn's view.

When it had passed, she had vanished.

What to do? No point in chasing her. Besides, he could not leave Mr. Holmes.

He turned back to the stoop.

Mr. Holmes was now standing in the doorway. He motioned Flynn to come up the steps and inside, shutting the outer door once Flynn was in the vestibule.

Flynn held out the watch to Mr. Holmes. "She gave me this—"

Mr. Holmes held up his finger for silence and looked at the watch, turning it over and inspecting the inscription.

He spoke quietly. "Tell me everything." he said.

10. WATSON

Waiting in the same room with Rexford became more and more uncomfortable. Plainly, the factory owner's patience had worn thin. He was standing before our settee, putting on his overcoat.

And then suddenly Holmes returned.

Rexford faced Holmes, his eyes blazing.

Holmes held out a gold watch.

Rexford's expression turned to one of astonishment.

Holmes said, "This is yours, I believe. The engraving proclaims as much."

Rexford gaped. "Where did you get this?"

"From someone who claims to know the thief. I may have more to say on that in the future, but for now I do not."

"You are indeed quite a marvel, Mr. Holmes."

"Nothing marvellous was involved. When do you last remember using the watch?"

"Only yesterday."

"In your office?"

"At the works, yes."

"Where, specifically, and for what purpose?"

A moment's reflection. "I was in the mixing house. I was observing the process of loading the mixed product into canvas sacks."

"What happens to the canvas sacks?"

"They are placed on a cart and sent to the green charge house."

"And how many men were working in the mixing house?"

"Only two. One to load the sack—"

"How?"

"Why, with a wooden shovel. To prevent sparks."

"And the other man?"

"He holds the sack open for the man with the shovel."

"Were you satisfied with their speed?"

"Actually, I was not. I told them we would need to produce at a faster rate if we were to meet our quota. You see, our orders have—"

Holmes held up a hand. "Where do you keep the watch when you retire for the night?"

"On my dressing table."

"And this morning?"

"It was not there."

"Can you clearly recall putting the watch on your dressing table last night?"

A long moment of hesitation. "I cannot."

"Please describe your movements yesterday evening."

"I had supper with my son. It was a late supper, because I had been occupied with work in the office. He kindly waited for me."

"What time did you begin dining?"

"Around eight-thirty."

"And how did you note the time?"

"Ah, I see, you are asking if I had my watch in my possession at that moment. But there is a tall clock in our entry hall, and I recall seeing the time there."

"And after your supper?"

"We each had a glass of cognac in the library."

"Only one glass?"

"I limit myself. Rex may have had two or three."

"What kind of cognac?"

"A French variety. Remy Martin."

"I know it. It comes in a very distinctive bottle. A blue bottle."

"No, you are mistaken there. The bottle is dark brown. Ordinary dark brown bottle glass."

"I will take your case."

Rexford gasped in surprise and happiness.

Holmes continued, ignoring the gasp and the proffered handshake of Mr. Rexford. "Watson and I will visit your facility this afternoon. My associate will also be there, if I can arrange for her to accompany us."

"Your associate?"

"Her name is Lucy James."

11. LUCY

Tobias Gregson was a tall, gangling man with large, square hands and a long face that even at the best of times was rather melancholy-looking. Today, though, I thought he looked especially haggard. Since last I'd seen him, he had grown a drooping, scraggly moustache, and he had the gaunt, hollow look of a man who's recently lost more weight than he had to spare.

Jack was entirely correct; Whitechapel was one of the city's most desperately poor—and thus most dangerously criminal—neighborhoods. A decade earlier, the Ripper killings had terrorized the district's fallen women, the most vulnerable who walked these streets, and the area was very little improved in terms of security since then.

We were meeting Gregson at one of the few locations where I'd felt safe in allowing Becky to accompany me. The Mile End Section House was the police equivalent of an army barracks, offering accommodation to all unmarried constables and sergeants.

We had found Gregson in the canteen room. It was now past noon, but luncheon was still being served to the officers who either had just come in from walking their beats, or else were about to depart on morning rounds. Police officers sat in groups around tables, eating from the platters of beef, boiled potatoes, and tea that were today's menu.

Gregson hadn't touched his own food, except to poke moodily at it with his fork. Instead, he sat hunched on the chair opposite mine, his shoulders slumped and lines of worry or exhaustion bracketing his eyes and the edges of his mouth.

"The Powder Island case." He looked from me to the note he held in one hand—the one Jack had written for me to give to him. A scowl pulled his lips down. "Can't say I see the point of digging up the past."

He glanced at the sergeant who was keeping watch on the men from the head of the room.

The sergeant was watching a friendly wrestling match going on in one corner—probably to gauge the odds of it remaining friendly—and didn't have any attention to spare for our table.

Despite the fact that he wore his blue tunic and constable's helmet and was clearly about to go on duty, Gregson took a hip flask out of his pocket, poured a hefty measure of what smelled like brandy into his teacup, then returned the flask to his pocket and tossed back half the drink in barely more than a single gulp.

"The case is over—finished." His voice was rough. "The Home Office investigated and wrote up their report. What else is there to say?"

"I don't know. But there must be something more to it. The owner of the factory requested a meeting with Holmes. He met with him at Baker Street this morning, in fact."

Becky and I had stopped in at 221B on our way to Whitechapel to deliver the news of the missing police file, and Holmes had given me a brief account of his meeting with Bradley Rexford.

Gregson nearly choked on another swallow of tea. "*Rexford's* trying to hire Mr. Holmes to re-open the investigation?"

"That surprises you?"

Gregson snorted. "He was about as much use to our investigation as a sick headache. So yes, it surprises me."

"Do you think it was Mr. Rexford who campaigned to get the investigation handed over to the Home Office?" I asked.

But Gregson's momentary flash of interest was gone. "Maybe—how do I know?" He stabbed viciously at the potatoes on his plate with his fork, shoveling them into his mouth. "Look, I don't know what more help I can give you, and I'm due on duty in five minutes. So if you don't mind, I'd like to finish my—"

He hadn't given me any help at all so far, but I doubted if pointing that out would do anything towards winning his favour.

It was Becky, though, who interrupted Gregson in the middle of his dismissal. "In *A Study in Scarlet*, you told Mr. Holmes, *you should never neglect any chance, however small it may seem.*"

"A Study in—" Gregson frowned. "Oh, the Enoch Drebber case. Yes, well. That was a long time ago." His expression had softened slightly as he looked at Becky, but now he wiped his mouth on the back of his hand, his jaw hardening as he stared down at his congealing slice of beef. "I've learned things since then."

"Such as?"

Gregson transferred his glower from his plate of food to me. "Such as, this world will punch you in the face if you let it."

His gaze was so bitter, I almost flinched.

I could understand. Gregson was still a relatively young man. He must have devoted himself to the job fiercely and tenaciously to have risen to the rank of Inspector in so short a time. He plainly wasn't married, or he wouldn't be occupying quarters here at the section house.

His entire life had been wrapped up in his career at Scotland Yard—and because of his very unwillingness to drop an investigation without learning the truth, he had lost everything.

It was a monumental injustice.

"Maybe," I said. "Sometimes, though, you get the chance to punch back."

There was a long moment where Gregson simply sat and stared at me, his long, melancholy face unreadable. Then, so quickly I might have imagined it, his lips curved up in the ghost of a smile.

"Well, if anyone were to get to the truth of the matter, it would be Mr. Holmes. And I can't think of a man who deserves to be slapped in the face with the truth more than Bradley Rexford. So what can I do?"

"You can tell me more about Mr. Rexford, to begin with. Why didn't he want you investigating the factory explosion?"

Gregson picked up his empty teacup, but then set it down with a frown and without reaching for the flask again. "Because there weren't any good answers, from his point of view. He didn't want to hear of any criminal cause, since a criminal could strike again and the factory wouldn't be safe. A man who makes the British army's gunpowder doesn't want to admit he's let an enemy get the better of him. Mind you, he didn't want the explosion chalked up to negligence, either. But to him, it was the lesser of the two evils. He could pin the blame on some hapless factory worker who'd supposedly been careless and let safety measures slip. Make an example of him by firing him, and then offer a lot of talk about how safety and good repair processes had been improved to prevent a recurrence, and how he'd every confidence in the new protocols they'd now got in place."

His voice was heavy with irony.

"Is that what brought you into Mr. Rexford's bad graces? Your unwillingness to pin the blame on a hapless factory worker's lack of care?"

"Partly." Gregson pushed the food around his place. "That and he'd got the wrong idea about …" His voice trailed off as he thought. "Well, never mind. Suffice it to say, we didn't see eye to eye on a good many things."

"And you definitely thought the explosion was a work of deliberate malice," I said. I'd already had Jack's account of the investigation, but I wanted to hear what Gregson would tell me. "Did you have any suspects?"

Gregson opened his mouth, then closed it again, shifting position in his chair.

"Nothing definite. I'd barely started collecting statements from witnesses before I was ordered to turn the file over to the Home Office man and drop the case."

I had the impression he'd started to say something, then changed his mind. If he did have suspicions, he wasn't going to share them with me. And pressing him, I was fairly sure, would only bring about a rapid end to this conversation.

"Lucy?" Becky had been studying the wresting match over the corner and now turned to me. "May I go over and watch?"

Either she was bored with Gregson's conversation—or else, more likely, she thought he would speak more freely without her there.

"Yes, all right."

She skipped off. Gregson watched her go, a frown between his brows. "She's Kelly's younger sister?"

"That's right." I watched without surprise as several of the uniformed constables obediently moved aside to let Becky enter the circle of spectators; Becky had that effect on even seasoned policemen. "You don't have to worry. She'll probably be giving the contestants pointers on their wrestling holds before too long."

Gregson's eyes lingered on Becky a moment, and then he cleared his throat. "Can I ask a question? No, wait, hear me out first." He raised his hand when I opened my mouth to answer. "I realise I've no right to ask Mr. Holmes for details about his meeting with Rexford. That'd be breaking his client's request for confidentiality. And I've no official right to be kept informed, the lord knows, since I've been kicked off the case. So, I won't ask for details. But let me just ask: have you any reason to think Rexford may have an enemy or two behind this affair?"

I thought of the second cab that seemed to have been waiting for Mr. Rexford at Baker Street—and the odd behaviour of the woman who had begged Flynn to return Mr. Rexford's watch.

Holmes had told me—briefly—about both incidents when he'd summed up the morning's meetings. But we'd had no time to discuss the implications.

"What makes you ask?"

Gregson's expression lightened briefly in a smile that made him look both younger and less careworn. "Because I've told you Mr. Rexford did his best to shut down our investigation. The next logical inference would be to ask whether I'd ever thought Rexford himself was behind the explosion and the supervisor's death—maybe he'd had a quarrel with the dead man, maybe he did it for the insurance money. But you haven't asked it, or even hinted that it's what you and Mr. Holmes are thinking. Therefore, you must have reason to think Rexford himself is threatened."

Holmes had been entirely right in his estimation of Gregson's abilities: Tobias Gregson was by no means a stupid man.

It was the Metropolitan Police who were stupid—criminal, even—letting his abilities be wasted on the duties of a beat constable.

"Whether or not he's in danger, I don't know for certain," I said carefully. "But I think it's fair to say that some unknown person or persons are keeping an eye on Mr. Rexford."

Gregson nodded, but lapsed into silence, his thoughts clearly running along their own complicated inner track.

"What about Mr. Rexford's son?" I asked.

Gregson looked up. "What about him?"

"Did he share his father's unwillingness to help with the investigation?"

Gregson jerked one shoulder. "I wouldn't say that. He was willing enough—or what for him counts as willing. But if young Mr. Rexford ever had a thought in his head that didn't revolve around himself or his precious yacht club, I'd be surprised."

I'd brought the Home Office Report with me from Baker Street and scanned it in the cab on the way here. I opened to a page somewhere in the middle, where the author of the report finally got around to saying something definite after pages and pages of verbosity. I said, "According to the Home Office, a possible cause of the accident is 'matches maliciously placed on the platform by person or persons unknown.'"

"Matches." Gregson snorted again. "Right. I heard about that. A couple of witnesses said they'd seen matches on the platform of another building. Miss Thiel—Bradley Rexford's niece—was one of them. But that was days before the explosion, and the weather was damp—it was damp on the day the place blew up, for that matter. There'd been a spell of rain just the night before. If the thick-headed sods at the Home Office think a few scattered wet matches were the cause of it ... well, they're even more lack-witted than I'd thought, or else—"

He stopped.

"Or else they've been either bribed or threatened into accepting the matches as a convenient explanation?" I suggested.

Gregson forked another bite of potato into his mouth and shrugged, one-sided, avoiding my gaze.

I waited a moment, then said, quietly, "So if I were to tell you that all of your files—notes, witness reports, everything else—are missing from Scotland Yard—"

I stopped. Gregson's expression had gone slack with shock, the colour slowly ebbing out of his face.

"I'd say—" he didn't speak for a long moment. He cleared his throat, but when he spoke his voice was husky. "Your husband Sergeant Kelly's a good man. First class copper. If he keeps on with the kind of work he's done so far at the Yard, he'll be made an Inspector one day. But not if he crosses the wrong people."

"The wrong people being ..."

Gregson shook his head. He darted a look around as though seeking to make sure we weren't being overheard, then leaned in across the table. "I've said all I'm going to. Maybe I've been knocked down to a beat constable—but at least I'm still alive." He pushed away his plate and stood up, once again not meeting my gaze. "Take it from me, it's something to be thankful for. Now if you'll excuse me, I need to start on my afternoon rounds."

12. WATSON

"We spoke with Gregson about the case," Lucy said. "He believes there was a police conspiracy to quash the investigation."

Holmes grimaced. Then he said, "We have time to catch the next train to Hounslow Heath. Can you come with us?"

Becky asked, "Where is Flynn?"

"Downstairs, in Mrs. Hudson's kitchen," I said. "He's getting breakfast, and then he's going to a cab station to interview a cabbie in a red scarf. The passenger in the cab may be connected with the explosion case."

"I'll be right back," Becky said, and ran down the stairs.

"She'll want to go with Flynn," Lucy said.

"Is that wise?" I asked.

"After meeting Gregson," she replied, "I'd like to keep Becky as far away from Powder Island as we can manage."

* * *

So Becky stayed behind with Flynn. Letting Flynn and Becky loose in the city on their own was often an invitation to disaster. But they had sworn they were only going to the cab station, which I thought would limit their opportunities for getting into trouble.

During the hour-long train journey, Lucy told us more of her meeting with Gregson, and how wearied and worn down the demoted Inspector had become in his reduced circumstances.

"A pity he was treated so unfairly for taking an interest in the case." I said.

Holmes said, "Perhaps we can put things right."

Lucy asked, "What is our plan?"

"Watson and I will question the employees at the factory. I should like you to go to the church in the village, where a celebration of the factory re-opening is being prepared. Parishioners are more likely to speak freely with you than they would with Watson and me."

"I'll see what I can learn."

We arrived at the Hounslow Heath station shortly afterward. There we said goodbye to Lucy. Holmes whispered something to her as he closed the door to her cab.

Holmes then asked me to arrange for a cab while he placed a telephone call to London. I did not hear the conversation, but my curiosity overtook me when we were in our cab, on the way to the other side of the Thames and the Rexford works. "Who did you call?" I asked.

"My friends at Lloyd's," he replied.

"Why?"

"They run the Registry of Ships."

"I do not understand the connection."

"There is no need. It may come to nothing."

We could see most of the factory buildings as our cab approached. They were stone, each distanced from the next. The stones were blackened with layers of soot accumulated over the years. We dismounted from our cab and found ourselves at the base of a footbridge across the river from the mainland, facing a wrought iron entrance gate and a stone guard shed.

A grey-haired man with a military bearing emerged from the

guard shed. "You'll be Mr. Holmes and Dr. Watson," he said, looking us up and down with an approving eye. "I've heard about you. And Mr. Rexford told us you'd be coming. Fairchild's the name. Naval Lieutenant till 1870, and here for the past thirty years. Do you have matches on your persons? If so, I would trouble you to empty them from your pockets and leave them with me."

"Company policy?" asked Holmes, as he handed over his box of safety matches.

"And strictly enforced, you may rest assured."

"The more so since the explosion, I'd expect," I said.

Fairchild shook his head, his brow furrowing between bushy white eyebrows. "I've been the enforcer, and I have not altered our procedures. No one passes through here carrying matches."

"But the Home Office report—"

"Pack of trumped-up nonsense. Said matches had been found days before the explosion. But they weren't dangerous."

"Why?" Holmes asked.

"Wet weather," Fairchild said. "But you gentlemen will make up your own minds. The office is the next building on your right. Miss Amy is expecting you."

"Miss Amy is Rexford's niece?" asked Holmes.

Fairchild nodded. "Amy Thiel." He looked at each of us in turn. "Stay on your guard. She has a sharp tongue, and I wouldn't be quick to rely on her."

"Did she tell the police that matches had been found?" I asked.

He shook his head. "I don't tell tales. Just a word to the wise. And you can pick up your own matches when you're ready to leave. I'll be here."

* * *

At my knock, Miss Amy Thiel looked up sharply from her desk. "Yes?"

Holmes spoke calmly. "Good afternoon, Miss Thiel. I am Sherlock Holmes, and this is Dr. Watson. Your uncle came to see me in London this morning."

She stood up quickly, walking briskly around her desk to stand before it, and then leaned back. Her blonde hair was neatly bound up into a bun atop her head in the fashion of the time. Dressed in black, she radiated a nervous tension, but she remained silent.

Holmes said, "We have come about the explosion, as I expect your uncle has told you."

She gave a curt nod. "My uncle telephoned that you would be coming. I do not understand why he wants to rake up the past, but there you are. He is the owner, after all."

She motioned us to the two wooden chairs facing her, and we sat. She remained standing, still leaning back against the desk. I had the impression that by standing she hoped to maintain a superior position. Or possibly there were papers on the desk she did not wish us to see.

Holmes asked, "Have you read the Home Office report?"

"Worthless," she said. "I hope we agree on that point. I believe the investigator thought he was being paid by the word. It is the quintessential blather of a government bureaucrat."

"You have some experience with bureaucrats?"

"Mr. Holmes, we are the largest gunpowder factory in Europe, and we sell most of our product to the British government. You can imagine the bureaucratic paperwork I must deal with every day."

"Indeed. Where were you at the time of the explosion?"

"I was in church. With my mother. In the second-row pew, behind Rex and his father. It was during the morning prayer when we heard the sound. We had just recited the words asking for salvation for the souls of others. I have tried to take some consolation in that, since it was the exact moment my father's soul had gone to meet his maker."

"What happened next?"

"Glass from the windows broke and fell. There was a general panic. My uncle and Rex ran for the entrance. I followed them, and saw them on the downstream bridge running towards the factory."

"You have had a great deal of work to do, since then."

"Yes, my uncle appointed Rex as my father's replacement, and I needed to teach him an enormous amount about our operations. Also, we had to build a new glazing-house, and other buildings had to be modified so we could continue production on a reduced basis. With less income, we had to lay off workers and reassign others. There was a significant amount of paperwork for those activities, which were in addition to all the usual operations."

"Difficult for you," I said.

"But important to the defense of England. So there really wasn't any choice."

"Do you get along with Rex?" Holmes asked.

"He is my cousin. We were childhood friends."

"How does he strike you—suited to the work?"

"He seems to have taken to it. A surprise to all. Before the explosion, he took little interest in the business. More interested in his friends at the yacht club and taking jaunts with his yacht."

"He fancies himself a sailor?"

"Well, he's given that up. At least he says he has. When he stops coming to work in his captain's hat, then we'll know it really is a new Rex." She gave an ironic smile, and then looked upwards, towards the doorway behind where Holmes and I were seated. "I see the postman coming," she said. "And my uncle is just behind him. Will you excuse me for a moment? I have some letters going out."

Holmes stood. I stood beside him. I noticed Holmes's gaze was directed to the desktop as Miss Thiel gathered up a stack of letters.

The topmost envelope was addressed to the Western Assurance Company office in London.

13. LUCY

My cab drew to a halt outside the modest stone parish church of St. Andrews, in Twickenham.

"Miss James?" A woman came out from the shadow of the church's vestry to meet me, her hand extended in greeting. "Or perhaps you prefer Mrs. Kelly?"

I smiled. The palpable sense of fear that had rolled off Gregson during our meeting had all my nerves tight with uneasiness. His words felt like sharp-edged rocks, rattling inside my head. *I'm still alive. Take it from me, it's something to be thankful for.*

But there was nothing I could do for the moment save to put all of that aside and give my full attention to the investigation at hand.

"Either is fine."

The other woman looked me up and down. She was dressed in black, tall and stocky, with red hair going grey at the temples. "I am Janice Thiel. Brad Rexford's sister." She added, with another searching glance at me, "It's unusual to meet a woman investigator."

"Perhaps." I had learned a long time ago that, contrary to what the suffragettes' campaigns would have people believe, the harshest critics of my choice of employment were often other women rather than men—and that the only way to confront their disapproval was to meet it head-on. "But your daughter works at the gunpowder factory as Mr. Rexford's personal clerk, doesn't she? That's rather unusual."

Mrs. Thiel sighed, her shoulders slumping as any challenge seemed to die out of her. "Amy, yes. Although I wish to heaven I could persuade her to give up the work. She won't hear of it, though. She is too much her father's daughter. And Brad has been good to both Amy and me, of course. Kind enough to allow us to live in the Dower House at Rexford Hall—though that keeps her close to him when he wants to discuss business matters away from the factory. He's even set up a little office in the main Hall just for her."

Across the river, on Powder Island, Holmes and Watson were paying a visit to the actual gunpowder factory. My own assigned task, though, was to interview the local residents in an effort to find any other eyewitness accounts of the explosion.

Although the odds that those accounts would contain anything of value were depressingly slim. Nine months after the incident, any witnesses who appeared at this point were likely to be of the attention-seeking variety, happy to swear they'd seen a dozen sinister-looking strangers swimming across the river with sticks of dynamite clenched between their teeth, if they thought it likely to gain them a few minutes' fame.

Now, a grey-haired man emerged from the church door behind us, interrupting before Janice Thiel could go on. "Mrs. Thiel? Where do you want the banners and bunting hung?"

"Oh—yes, thank you, John." Mrs. Thiel turned, looking flustered. "There, on the outside of the church hall will be fine."

"Right you are."

The man vanished back inside the church, and Mrs. Thiel turned back to me. "Do you mind if we stay outside? We can be private, but there is to be a potluck supper here tomorrow night—in celebration of the new building opening over at the factory. I really ought to keep an eye on things."

"Of course."

I kept my voice level, but my pulse quickened as I recalled the words of the anonymous note Holmes had shown me on the train journey.

Don't be too quick to celebrate. Another big bang is coming your way.

Two men came out of the church—John, and one other—carrying a ladder between them, and started to hang large, brightly painted banners in the colours of the Union Jack flag along the side of the church hall.

Largest in Europe ... We are Proud ... Remain Largest ... Safety is Our Guide.

"We used to hold these occasions monthly, but this is the first potluck supper we've held since the accident," Mrs. Thiel said. The worry etched on her face was more pronounced as she watched the men at work. "The livelihood of a good many of the parishioners depends on the factory's success. And since the explosion, management has laid off some of the workers, and cut back the hours of nearly all that remained."

"It must have been a very difficult time for everyone."

"Yes. Although my brother-in-law has done his best to help. Brad took out a loan and personally guaranteed it in order to rebuild and provide the workers some semblance of wages. Amy tells me keeping the workforce reasonably intact is good business, of course. But it was still a kind gesture, and one the people here appreciate."

Mrs. Thiel looked back at the church, where more workers were bustling back and forth, carrying chairs and tables.

"Did you know Mr. Rexford was planning to consult Mr. Holmes this morning?"

Holmes had suggested I ask, hoping to learn how the man in the conspicuous captain's cap and cape might have known of Rexford's visit.

"I?" Mrs. Thiel shook her head. "No. I suppose Bradley would have told my daughter—since it meant he would be absent this morning from the factory. But neither of them told me." A twist of pain or perhaps sadness crossed her expression. "I suppose they thought it would upset me, to hear the investigation was being re-opened."

I hesitated, wondering how to phrase the next question. "There is a witness who claims to have seen Mr. Rexford at a gin shop in the East End of London. A place called the Blue Bottle."

"Bradley?" Mrs. Thiel's eyes opened wide with astonishment.

"That surprises you?"

"So much so that I would say your witness must have been mistaken. It is not just a question of Bradley's morals—although I have never known him to be unfaithful to the memory of his wife. It is also his very character. Bradley is a man who appreciates his creature comforts. He likes the best of everything—the finest wines and cigars, the most well-tailored clothes. The thought of him voluntarily going to an unsavoury grog shop in the east end ... well," she exhaled a half-laugh. "It's so absurd as to be almost impossible."

"What about Mr. Rexford's son?"

"Young Rex?" Mrs. Thiel gave me a sharp glance. "Are you asking whether Rex is more likely to attend a lower-class establishment than his father?"

"No offence meant." Mrs. Thiel's tone of voice gave me the answer, decidedly in the affirmative. "But I understand Mr. Rexford's son is now the new factory supervisor? You called him Rex?"

"Yes. Of course, he is actually Bradley Rexford III, after his father and grandfather. But he has always gone by the nickname." The line of Mrs. Thiel's mouth had tightened perceptibly.

"You don't like him?"

"Not exactly. I—well." Mrs. Thiel exhaled a sharp breath and gave me a glance that held a brief flash of wry amusement. When she was not desperately worried, Janice Thiel was probably a very likable woman. "I'm not accustomed to speaking of private family matters to complete strangers. But it is pointless to hire an investigator and then refuse to give her the information she requires in order to investigate. A waste of expenditures, my daughter would probably call it. Or something of the sort. I usually get these accounting terms all wrong." She smiled briefly, then went on, "To be blunt, then, it is not that I dislike Rex. I doubt anyone could actively dislike him. I have known him from his earliest childhood, and he has always been a dreamer—no head for practical matters and very little taste for unpleasant tasks or responsibility. He was always playing at practical jokes. He had a wooden catapult, I remember—one of those toys boys love, the sort that fire small pebbles. He would hide in an upstairs window and use it to knock the feathers off the hats of fine ladies who came to visit his mother for tea—and yet it was difficult to be angry with him, he was such a happy, merry child. No, I like Rex well enough. I simply do not wish to have him for a son-in-law."

My eyebrows rose. As a part of bringing me up to date on the details of the case, Holmes had filled me in on the Rexford family background. But this was the first I had heard of a possible attachment between Amy Thiel and Bradley Rexford's son.

"And do you think it likely that your daughter will marry Rex?" I asked.

Our conversation was straying a fair distance away from the explosion at the factory. But it was one of Holmes's cardinal rules of investigation that one should always let a witness talk who was willing to do so. One never knew when an important detail might be revealed in the midst of seeming trivialities.

"I don't know." Mrs. Thiel looked troubled once again. "Girls today are so different from what we were in my young days—or perhaps it is only Amy who is different from what I was at her age. I cannot tell whether she cares for Rex at all. She is very … 'hard' isn't quite the word. Practical. Amy is all practicality and business and good sense. I'm afraid sometimes she might marry Rex simply because she believes it would make good business sense to do so—keeping the factory entirely within the family."

"And does Rex wish to marry her for the same reasons?"

"Rex?" Mrs. Thiel looked startled. "Oh no. No, I believe he cares for Amy quite genuinely. He has from the time they were young. And he was hardly business-like back then. His dream was to have the factory sponsor a big racing yacht, like Mr. Lipton's, which is just foolishness, if you know anything about the costs involved. Before he went away to school, he spent most of his time at the yacht club, or on his own little sailboat, out on the river. Then when he came back, he talked his father into buying a bigger boat that he docked at the club. He called it a yacht, though it was far smaller than most of the boats at the club, and nothing to compare with the big racing yachts. But he never took it out to sea. Then he sold it, just before the explosion. But he hasn't stopped wearing that captain's cap."

The back of my neck prickled. "Was he here this morning?"

Mrs. Thiel looked mildly startled. "Why, yes. Is it important?"

"Likely not."

Except that a captain's cap had been worn by the man whom Flynn had tailed this morning.

If it had been Rex, though, that begged the question of why he would have chosen to spy on his own father.

Mrs. Thiel went on, "Rex sold his 'yacht' last year, because he said the factory had some financial troubles and needed new capital to invest in new equipment." She gave another faint smile. "Then came the explosion. So the new equipment never was purchased. Whatever he received for the yacht was far less than what the factory needed. Though I suppose it is the thought that counts."

"But you still do not wish for Amy to marry him."

"No." Mrs. Thiel's voice hardened. "Rex may have genuinely changed and matured. I hope he has. He has proven a more capable supervisor than anyone would have supposed. Just this morning, he was here early—before going in to work at the factory—delivering pastries from the Rexford Hall kitchen to be served at the potluck supper. But still—" Mrs. Thiel gave a small, frustrated shake of her head. "I don't know, perhaps it is unreasonable of me not to trust him. Many young men sow their wild oats, as the saying goes, and then settle down to a life of sober respectability. But at a minimum, I cannot help feeling Amy and Rex's temperaments are utterly unsuited to one another as marriage partners."

"A short while ago, you spoke of the explosion as an accident. Is that what you believe?" I asked.

Mrs. Thiel pleated a fold of her skirt between two fingers, her lower lip caught between her teeth. "I don't know." She looked up at me. "I will tell you, though, that on that terrible morning, I had the most powerful feeling of dread." She looked around her with a kind of dazed pain in her eyes. "I was actually here, at church, when we heard the horrid sound."

I hesitated. Mrs. Thiel's husband had lost his life in that very same explosion.

I'd confronted murderers intent on adding me to their list of victims—many of them. But this was always the hardest part of an investigation.

"I'm sorry to make you speak of it," I began.

"It's all right." Mrs. Thiel's mouth twisted in a fractured smile that, this time, held no humour at all. "Heaven knows I have relived it often enough in my own mind. Speaking of it cannot make it hurt more than it already does—or alter the fact that Marcus is gone. What is it you wish to know?"

"Anything at all you can tell me. I know it is months ago—"

Mrs. Thiel interrupted. "I remember—I remember everything, every detail of that awful day. As I said, I had the most terrible sense of foreboding that morning. It was almost like an illness. I couldn't shake the feeling that something dreadful was to occur. I even begged Marcus to come here, to church with me, instead of going to the factory as he usually did. But he wouldn't hear of it, of course." Her voice wavered, and she stopped, wiping her eyes. "Marcus was so passionate about having risen to manage the operation of the factory. He worked his way up from a messenger boy. He felt obligated to set an example for the other workers. They had been wanting their wages increased, and Marcus kept saying that they couldn't expect any rise in pay if they weren't living up to their end of the bargain to help the business prosper. And now ... now Amy is just like him. Just as hard-headed, just as driven. But you were asking about the explosion." She took a steadying breath and seemed to collect herself. "We were inside the church sanctuary when it happened. If you come with me, I can show you."

St. Andrews was a small church, the sanctuary designed in a simple style of white plastered walls pointing the focus towards an arched stained-glass window above the vestry. Mrs. Thiel led the way to the front two pews.

"My daughter and I were sitting just here." She gestured. "And Rex and Bradley were here, in the pew in front, when it happened. We heard the explosion—so loud, it was like nothing I'd ever known before. It broke some of the stained glass windows in the sanctuary. And then, just a few moments later, we heard the church clock chiming the hour." She shivered, her eyes darkening at the memory. "It was like a death knell."

"So Bradley—" I started to ask, but stopped as a sudden shout of alarm came from outside the church.

"Dear heaven, what now?" Turning, Mrs. Thiel ran back up the aisle and out the door, and I followed, my heartbeat quickening.

Several of the workmen who had been hanging up banners huddled around another man who lay on the ground, clutching his leg and moaning.

"Looks to me his leg's broken, missus," one of the others told Mrs. Thiel. "And he can thank his lucky stars it's not his neck. Upper rung of the ladder broke under him when he was working at hanging up the bunting."

Mrs. Thiel had gone very pale. "But that's Paul Jeffries! He's engaged to be married to my daughter's maid. Paul!"

She hurried forwards to kneel at the injured man's side.

The rest of the workmen grouped around them, discussing arrangements for who should be sent to fetch a doctor and whether a makeshift stretcher could be constructed from the chairs inside. Mrs. Thiel was insisting the man be brought to Rexford Hall, which apparently was not far away, and asking someone to use the village telephone to send word to that effect.

But I listened to the talk with only half an ear. No one was paying any attention either to me or to what I assumed was the faulty ladder, which now lay on its side near the church's outer wall.

I approached and crouched down so I could examine the broken uppermost rung, running the tip of my finger across the splintered wood.

"Miss James!" Mrs. Thiel had remembered me and now called out, turning from the injured young man. "I'm terribly sorry to cut our interview short, but I must go with Paul to Rexford Hall to wait for the doctor."

I straightened up quickly. "It's all right. I entirely understand," I told her. "I'll go with you, if I may."

"Oh—yes, of course." Mrs. Thiel gave a distracted nod, and I moved further away from the ladder—I hoped before anyone else had seen me examining it.

An upper rung had broken, true. But it had first been neatly cut, sawed nearly through so that only the very top of the wooden step remained intact.

It would have been primed to snap the moment any weight was placed on it.

14. WATSON

Holmes and I waited just inside the office building as the postman arrived. We saw him pick up the letters from Miss Thiel and give her more letters in return. She returned to her desk and began to sort out the day's mail deliveries.

Holmes and I waited outside as our client, Brad Rexford, approached. He was clad in the same heavy coat, hat and muffler he had worn for his visit in Baker Street, and he appeared ill at ease.

"Gentlemen," he said, "A private discussion, if you will. Could you step a bit farther away from the office?"

We did as he requested. He closed the door to the office without a word to Miss Thiel, who was still occupied with her letter sorting, and then stepped up to join us.

"I want to discuss financial matters," he said, looking around us as though worried our conversation would be overheard. "I should like to re-emphasize what people should know and what should remain private."

"We are at your service," Holmes said.

"First, my son Rex must not know of the proposed float of shares."

"Understood."

"Second, I have taken out a loan, in order to fund the rebuilding and remodelling required to operate in the interim. Proceeds from our insurance were not sufficient to cover those expenses. And our revenues were reduced, since we had to operate at reduced capacity after the destruction of our lower glazing house."

"Understandable," Holmes said.

"My son Rex knows about the loan. However, he does not know the loan is secured by a mortgage against the family estate not far from here. Rex lives there with me."

Holmes nodded. "So if the business fails, both of you lose your homes."

Rexford nodded. "I was not sure my boy could function properly, if he knew the risk involved in the decisions he had to make daily."

"He appears to have succeeded thus far," I said.

"Yes, he has. So I don't want him to know about the mortgage."

"We quite understand."

"The boy has given up a lot. It's more or less been all work and no play for him these days."

"And your niece says he has given up his yachting activities," I said.

"More than that. He sold his yacht. About a year ago we needed money to buy new equipment, and he gave up the yacht. Handled the sale himself. And then the explosion happened, so we had to use the proceeds to rebuild. But he hasn't complained, and he hasn't gone back to the yacht club. Why—"

Rexford broke off. Outside the gate, a very ornate and expensive carriage was rolling up to the guardhouse. A heavyset, florid-looking man got out.

Rexford's expression darkened. "Fairchild!" he shouted to the guard. "Keep the gate shut. Don't let that snake come a step further!"

He turned to us. "It's Jerrard. He owns a rival gunpowder works. Not as good as ours, but he's always hoping to cause trouble."

"I heard you, Rexford," said the florid-faced man, standing at the gate. He waved a document in one hand. "You owe me five hundred pounds, and it's due today. Give me my money!"

"Get off my property!"

Jerrard sneered, his face up against the bars. "Either you pay up or I'll foreclose. Then I'll come here any time I like, because I will be the owner."

"Over my dead body!"

"That would be a bonus!"

By now, the gatekeeper was behind Jerrard, about to place a hand on Jerrard's shoulder.

"Throw the man out!" screamed Rexford.

"No need for that," Jerrard said, moving away, and giving a final wave of the document. "I'll be off to court now, and the sheriff will be around to evict you, Rexford!"

He climbed back into his carriage and drove off.

"He's wasting his time," said Rexford, turning to Holmes. "I could pay the little swine today, but there is a grace period in the loan. I refuse to give him my money a minute sooner than absolutely necessary."

"Why are you both so emotional about a business matter?"

"He has blackened my reputation."

"How so?"

"Making false claims about defects in my products. The man has no principles."

"Though he did loan you five hundred pounds?"

"When I was in dire straits, just after the explosion, yes he did. But he did not make the loan out of kindness. He hopes to ruin my reputation so my company revenues will drop and I will fail to pay."

Then we heard a young man's voice. "Ahoy there!"

We saw a tall youth in a dark wool cape and white captain's cap approaching on one of the pathways within the factory campus.

"Ah," said Rexford. "There's my son. I've asked him to give you a tour of the property."

15. FLYNN

The cabstand was busy at this time of day, when rich people were either driving home from luncheons or going out to pay afternoon calls. Only two cabs were parked in the eleven available spaces, and the cab master was busy barking orders at a couple of men who were tending to a horse that had thrown one of its shoes.

Flynn had the number of the cab driven by the man in the red scarf, which meant he'd found out the fellow's name without too much trouble: John Todd. The harried-looking cab master had stopped barking orders long enough to wave at a man inside the small wooden shelter where the cabbies could rest from the cold or take a bite of food between searching for fares.

"He's actually here—that's lucky," Becky murmured, as they approached the shelter.

"I suppose." Flynn could see through the open doorway of the shelter that John Todd wore a red scarf, so he was pretty sure it was the same man.

But he couldn't shake an uneasy feeling that had been nagging at him since they'd left Baker Street.

It was the same feeling he'd had a week ago, when he'd been jumped and kidnapped while out on a job like this for Mr. Holmes. And the worst of it was, he couldn't be sure whether the uneasiness was real, and something he should pay attention to. Or just leftovers from being tied up and stuffed inside a steamer trunk for hours on end.

Flynn shoved the memories back, wishing he could stuff them inside the same kind of trunk.

But he couldn't stop himself from asking Becky, "Do you have a feeling something's wrong?"

"Wrong?" At least Becky didn't tell him he was crazy—or getting to be afraid of his own shadow. "How do you mean?"

"I don't know." Flynn exhaled a breath of frustration. He didn't like being scared—and he especially didn't like not being able to put his finger on why he should feel that way. "I just keep feeling like there's something …" he glanced back at the street behind them, which was busy, too.

Omnibuses and wagons, shoppers, day labourers with picks and shovels over their shoulders—all were slogging through the dirty slush remaining from this morning's snowfall.

"You think someone is following us?" Becky asked.

"I don't know." Flynn frowned, trying to decide what about the street scene struck him as wrong. Or if there really was anything wrong.

A couple of vendors had set up shop near the cabstand: a knife sharpener, who was holding knives against his big spinning wheel, and a fruit vendor. The fruit vendor wasn't likely to have much luck; most of the apples he was selling looked half rotten.

Becky frowned, too, and looked like she might be starting to feel a bit jumpy, too. But then she shook her head. "Well, let's question the cab driver, and then we can work out whether anyone really is watching us."

Inside the shelter, cabman John Todd hunched over a plate of boiled rabbit and pickled pork, and only grunted without looking up when Flynn asked if they could talk to him.

"It's a free country—or used to be."

"Do you remember taking a fare to Baker Street station earlier today?" Flynn asked.

The cabbie coughed, wiped his mouth, and looked up at them.

"Drive a lot o' fares all over the city." He coughed again and gave a gusty sigh. "Wind, rain, perishing cold, don't matter, still got ter be out there on top o' the cab. Don't pay any of 'em much mind—unless they don't pay."

His gloomy expression suggested this happened often. Although that could have just been his usual look. He was an older man, with a wrinkled, leathery face that made Flynn think of a walnut: just as hard, just as deeply furrowed. Deep frown lines ran down from the edges of his mouth almost to his bristly chin.

"You took this fare from 221B Baker Street to the station," Flynn said.

John Todd gave a grunt that could have meant anything from *yes* to *no idea* to *go away and let me eat in peace.*

"Can you remember anything about him?" Becky asked.

The cabbie looked up again, wheezing. For a second, Flynn was worried the man was having some kind of a fit, but then he realised the sound was what for John Todd passed as laughing.

"Oh, yeah." He blew his nose on the end of his scarf. "Make all of my fares sit for a portrait, I do, so I can be sure to remember what they look like."

Perfect, Flynn thought sourly. A down-in-the-mouth, sarcastic cab driver: exactly what they needed.

"This man was wearing a white captain's hat and a dark cape," Becky said. She dug into her pocket and brought out a sixpence—although she had sense enough not to hand it over yet. "And he may have been mixed up with something criminal. Do you remember him?"

Outside on the street, a blue uniformed police constable trudged past on his rounds. Maybe it was the sight of the police that made the cabbie more cooperative, or maybe it was the sixpence.

John Todd didn't ask what Becky meant by something criminal, but he scratched his chin, his eyes on the coin in her hand. "Maybe I do remember him now. Fat chap. Squeaky kind of voice."

"Squeaky?"

"High pitched—like maybe he'd got a touch of the croup. No surprise in this cold."

"Can you remember where you picked him up?" Flynn asked.

"Where was it, now?" The cabbie screwed up his face in an effort of remembrance. "I don't know as how I can recollect that."

Becky looked at Flynn, tilting her head to ask a silent question. Flynn nodded. He'd bet more than a sixpence they weren't going to get any more useful information by hanging about here—and the uneasy prickling feeling on his neck was back, making him want to keep moving.

Becky dropped the coin into the cabbie's hand.

"Piccadilly Station," John Todd said promptly. "Picked him up at Piccadilly."

16. WATSON

"I'd like to take you to our shot tower," said young Rexford when he had reached us at the factory office entrance. "You'll have a better view of the whole operation from there."

The young man's reddish-brown hair was barely visible beneath his white captain's cap. He had inherited his father's sturdy frame and commanding stature, but he was leaner, and his facial features were still clean-shaven and raw-boned. He moved forcefully, as though to demonstrate his position of leadership.

We followed.

After a brief trek through the snow, we reached the entry door to a tall tower, possibly one hundred feet tall. "Like a lighthouse, don't you think?" young Rexford said. "Come inside." He made a sweeping gesture, as though leading us into battle. "Onwards and upwards!"

We entered the tower and climbed up the massive stone circular staircase built against the thick stone interior walls. The centre of the great tower was an empty, hollow column. Daylight from a glass cupola above us illuminated the steps. When we reached the top, we stood on a stone platform with glassed-in windows all around.

As young Rex had foretold, the vantage point gave a good view of the snowy landscape and the factory buildings below.

"This tower was built by our family seventy years ago," Rex said. "Originally they used it for gunshot manufacture. Highly ingenious." He pointed to a basin hollowed-out from the stone platform. "They poured molten lead into that basin. Then they scooped it out and let the liquid drop from the basin. The lead fell nearly a hundred feet, down through the hollow core you see beneath you, and as it fell it separated into droplets, like rain. The droplets then landed in a water tank on the floor below. They cooled in the water into perfectly round little spheres, and formed gunshot pellets. So to this day, this building where we stand is called the Shot Tower."

Rex looked at us, obviously proud of his family business.

"Interesting," I said, out of politeness. Holmes remained silent.

"We don't make gunshot pellets here anymore," young Rex went on. "But we do use this building as a lookout tower. From these windows we can view any building in our operation, and if we see a fire hazard, we can give a prompt warning. I like to come up here and think about the future. My father and I have some great planning sessions right up here in this very spot."

Holmes asked, "Where were you when the explosion occurred?"

"Hasn't my father told you? I was with him in church. The explosion happened just during Morning Prayers." Rex pointed towards the window. "You can see the church right across the river."

We stood closer to the window. The river made a great black curving swath through the partially snow-covered countryside. A small stone church stood on the far riverbank.

"You can see the rooftops of all our buildings from up here. We keep the operations separate, for safety purposes, so one explosion doesn't destroy everything else on this side of the river, or harm the public on the other."

Holmes said, "Where did the explosion occur?"

"Right where the new building is now, the one where the stones and the roof slates haven't darkened with age. That's the part of the operation we're about to reopen. The glazing house."

"I see it is quite close to the river, with its own dock," said Holmes. "Do you think Mr. Jerrard could have set off the explosion?"

Rex looked shocked by the idea. He was silent. Then he asked, "How?"

"By boat, I would think. Jerrard or his associate might drift downstream in a small boat, with a dynamite charge of some kind. The dynamite could have a long fuse, giving the perpetrator time enough to get back in his boat and row out of harm's way."

Rex said, "You certainly are a clever one, Mr. Holmes. And you may have just solved the mystery! This will be a great relief to my father. Will you bring in the police now, and have Jerrard arrested?"

For a long moment, Holmes gazed down at the river waters far below. He seemed to be considering the idea. Then he shook his head. "I think not. Not just yet. We shall need more evidence."

17. FLYNN

"Where do we go now?" Becky asked when they were back on the street, outside the cabman's shelter. "Should we try asking at Piccadilly Station, do you think?"

Flynn shook his head. "Waste of time. Busy station like that, no one notices anything."

"Do we just go back to Baker Street, then?"

Part of Flynn wanted to—anything to get off this street. Which was exactly why he couldn't. If he lost his nerve, he'd be no good to Mr. Holmes or anyone else.

"There's still the Blue Bottle."

"The what?"

"The Blue Bottle. The place where the cockney woman said her friend had met Mr. Rexford and nicked his watch."

Becky was frowning, watching the fruit vendor who seemed to have given up and was now wheeling his cartload of rotten apples away up the street.

"Do you think she was telling the truth?" she finally asked.

"Don't know." There'd been something funny about the woman, although Flynn couldn't quite put his finger on what. But then he was getting good and sick of uneasy feelings he couldn't identify. Maybe the woman had been speaking the gospel truth. "Seems like it's worth looking into, though—see if anyone at the Blue Bottle knows if Mr. Rexford's a regular customer there."

Becky was still frowning, like she was thinking about something else. But she said. "All right. Do we walk or take a cab?"

Flynn took one last look up and down the street, which still looked just as ordinary as ever. "Cab," he said. He still wanted to get away from here as fast as possible. "Maybe we can get John Todd to take us, once he's finished eating."

John Todd hadn't been the first cabbie available, but another driver brought them to the East End, and Becky paid him before hopping out of the carriage. She eyed the gin shop doubtfully.

The Blue Bottle was a funny name for the place, she thought. East-enders sometimes called the police blue bottles. But from the look of the gin shop with the name in dirty gold letters over the door, it was the sort of place where people who wanted to stay far, far away from the coppers would go.

The outside walls were cracked and dirty, with piles of dirt and rubbish heaped against them. A pair of dead rats lay in the muddy gutter just next to the door, and half the windows were either broken or else boarded up.

"Mr. Rexford is a regular customer *here*?" Becky said.

Flynn shrugged, kicking a rusty tin can back towards the rubbish heap it had rolled from. "So the girl said."

Sometimes rich blokes did come down to drink and carouse down here in the poor neighborhoods. Slumming, they called it. Flynn had seen them. They thought it was all a big laugh or an adventure.

Mr. Rexford hadn't struck Flynn as that sort, just from the quick look Flynn had got of him, but you never knew.

"Were we followed here, do you think?" Becky asked.

"Can't tell." Flynn still felt jumpy, but then in a neighbourhood like this one, you'd be stupid *not* to keep your eyes open and your wits about you. "I didn't see anyone behind us in the cab, anyway," he said.

There weren't so many people about here, either. A pony-drawn rag and bone cart rumbled by. Across the street, a pair of flower vendors were quarrelling loudly over the rights to that particular street corner.

And closer by, there was a big, tough-looking boy a year or two older than Flynn selling cigars and cigarettes outside the gin shop. He had a tray looped around his neck with a bit of dirty rope and was scowling out at the world from under heavy brows.

"Where do we start?" Flynn asked.

Becky wasn't paying attention, though. She was frowning again, watching something up the road. Turning, Flynn saw a copper just turning the corner. It was getting to be late after-noon, with shadows closing in, and the police officer's helmet gleamed in the light from a gas lamp.

Flynn never would have thought he'd be glad to see a copper, but at the moment it was good to know that if they got into trouble, there'd be an officer of the law nearby.

"What did you say?" Becky asked.

"Do we go inside and ask about Rexford?"

Becky looked at the gin shop, considering. "I don't think we should bother, no one in there is likely to talk to us. They'll either laugh at us or try to rob us, but they won't be any help."

That was probably true, but it didn't get them any closer to finding out if Rexford had been here.

"We should ask him." Becky nodded to the boy selling cigars. "He looks like he probably sets up shop here often."

Flynn looked at the boy, who had shoulders like an ox and

hands that looked like a couple of cricket mitts—and who was glowering as if he hated the entire world.

"Oh good," Flynn said. "How'd you know I was just hoping for the chance to get punched in the nose?"

"He'd have to catch you first. He's strong, but he doesn't look as though he'd be very fast," Becky said. "At worst, we can always run away."

That didn't make Flynn feel a whole lot better. He watched as a man who'd clearly had one too many came staggering out of the gin shop, waved a coin in the cigar boy's face, and then went back inside after he'd bought a bag of snuff.

Flynn sighed. He didn't have any better ideas, and he didn't want to go back to Mr. Holmes empty-handed.

"How do we want to go about asking him? Do we have any more money?"

"It wouldn't work. He'd just pocket the money and either refuse to say anything or tell us a packet of lies. He's already cheating all his paying customers. That snuff he just sold the drunk man? It was half sawdust—I could tell even from all the way over here."

"All right, then. Divide and conquer?"

And hope the boy was as slow as Becky guessed.

"All right." Becky didn't look worried, anyway. She slipped off up the street, where the growing darkness made it even harder to keep track of her movements.

Flynn put his hands in his pockets and strolled over to the dark-haired boy.

"Hello there. I'm looking for my sister."

The boy's upper lip curled in a sneer. "Good fer you. 'Ow about you look somewhere else?"

"No call to get nasty." Flynn held up his hands. "I was just wondering if you might have seen her in the Blue Bottle there. Dark hair, tan color wool coat, grey linen scarf? Think she's been here?"

The boy's scowl deepened. "I fink you'd better get outa my sight, 'adn't you."

Flynn stood his ground. If you had to go up against someone stronger than you, do it with confidence, he always said.

"You must not like your teeth much, mate."

"What?" The boy's expression creased in momentary confusion. "What're you talking about?"

"Her." Flynn nodded to Becky, who'd come up behind the boy, and now took hold of the rope holding his tray of cigars and jerked, yanking him off his feet.

Flynn had to admit it was a satisfying sight. The boy fell over with a crash, landed flat on his back on the muddy cobblestones, and lay gaping up and them, his mouth opening and closing like a fish as he tried to get back the breath that had been knocked out of him.

"Let's try this again," Flynn said. "Unless you want me to kick your two front teeth out, you'll answer my questions: have you seen a dark-haired girl hanging around the Blue Bottle? Wears a lot of face paint, looks like she got dragged backwards through a hedge in Hyde Park?"

The boy looked tougher than he really was, because he didn't try to get up or fight back. Still wide-eyed and puffing for air, he shook his head. "Don't fink so. Only woman who works in the Blue Bottle is old Maud what scrubs the glasses—and she's about a 'undred, with a face like a bulldog."

"What about a Mr. Bradley Rexford?" Becky asked. "Is he

a regular customer here?"

The boy had recovered enough to give her the kind of look that said he couldn't believe how stupid she'd have to be to ask the question.

"And 'ow'd I know that? No one around here uses proper names."

Becky opened her mouth, but Flynn never got the chance to find out what she would have asked next, because someone screamed from further along the block.

Flynn's head jerked up and he stared through the grey dusk shadows, straining his eyes to see what had happened.

Becky gasped. "It's the police constable—look, he must have been hurt or taken ill."

Looking where she pointed, Flynn could see a man in a blue uniform lying on the ground. He'd have run as fast as he could in the opposite direction, but Becky had hopped up and was racing towards the crowd that had already gathered.

By the time Flynn had caught up to her, she had stopped short just a few feet away from the fallen copper, who was a tall, skinny fellow with a blond moustache and blond hair.

"What's wrong?" Flynn asked.

Becky looked like she'd just seen a ghost go swooping down the street. "That's Inspector—I mean Constable Gregson," she whispered. "I saw him just this morning with Lucy. And then I saw him walk past when we were at the cabstand—and again just now. He didn't come close enough for me to recognize him, but I thought he looked familiar. But then I thought maybe I was just imagining things!"

She bit her lip, looking over at Gregson.

He hadn't just been taken sick, that was certain. Flynn wasn't sure what had happened to him, but there was a dark, wet stain all down the front of his tunic. Blood.

"He was following *us*?" he asked.

"I don't know! Maybe. Is he still alive?"

Flynn couldn't tell that, either. Gregson wasn't moving, his eyes were closed—and he didn't look like he was aware of the crowd pressing in all around him.

A couple of the men who'd come running up—big, burly fellows who made the cigar boy they'd questioned look like a tame kitten—were crouching down and tugging Gregson's body, trying to roll him over.

"Think he's got anything valuable on him?" one asked.

The other one laughed harshly. "Never know. One thing, he can't arrest us for robbery, now can he? Not if he never wakes up."

"Stop!" Becky shouted.

Flynn wouldn't have gotten up and confronted the street toughs unless someone had held a gun to his head. He'd maybe have tried to rescue Gregson, but he would have tried a distraction first.

But Becky jumped right in between Gregson and the two men and faced them, her fists clenched and her eyes blazing fury.

"Get away from him! This man is a personal friend of Mr. Sherlock Holmes, and if you so much as touch him, Mr. Holmes will see to it that you spend the rest of your lives behind bars!"

Flynn didn't know if it was the mention of Mr. Holmes's name or if the men were just shocked at being told off by a girl. But they stopped, grunted, and then shuffled away. Pretty soon, the other onlookers did, too.

"He *is* still alive." Becky was feeling for the pulse in Gregson's neck. "But he needs help. Go and see if you can find another policeman, I'll stay with him here."

Flynn nodded. "All right." He stopped a second, though, looking down at the unconscious policeman. "What would he want to follow us for?"

"He worked the Rexford case. I heard him telling Lucy about it this morning. It's the reason he was demoted from Inspector to a beat constable. He must have thought there was a chance we could lead him to a clue."

"I guess it's good news if he was the one following us."

Flynn would rather have Gregson on his tail than whoever had planted a bomb and exploded a gunpowder factory.

"Maybe." Becky looked pale and scared as she tugged the folds of her coat more tightly around her. "I just realised something else, though. Remember that fruit vendor we saw outside the cabstand?"

It took Flynn a second to think back, but then he got it, too. His stomach dropped.

"His boots were new." He should have spotted it at the time.

"Exactly. Much too new. He'd never have been able to afford a pair like that with whatever he made selling half-rotten apples," Becky said.

"So, was he following us? Or Gregson?" Flynn nodded to the man still bleeding on the ground.

"I don't know." Becky shivered. "Just get help—and be careful."

Flynn's insides felt like they'd been scooped out and replaced with ice, but he nodded. "I'll get an ambulance. Then I'll send word to Jack so he can tell Mr. Holmes."

He took off up the street at a run.

18. LUCY

I was alone in the Rexford family carriage. Mrs. Thiel had elected to ride to Rexford Hall with the injured man in a farm cart, so she could sit alongside and help support his broken leg.

We drove up the sweep of gravel drive at the front of the Hall, a handsome building of red brick, with two wings flanking a central, gabled entrance, making the footprint of the house resemble the shape of a letter *E*.

Legend had it that Queen Elizabeth had considered it a delicate compliment and been more likely to bestow her royal presence on manors built with her initial in mind. Although from the large scale of the construction, and from the fresh-looking exterior, I thought Rexford Hall was a newer imitation rather than an authentic Elizabethan manor home.

A slender, fair-haired young woman, dressed in black, came hurrying out to meet us. She went straight to the cart, and I heard her issuing brisk orders to the workers who had ridden along.

"Yes, bring him straight inside—carefully, now. I have the sofa in the downstairs parlour all ready. Yes, mother, I've already telephoned for the doctor, he should be here any moment."

This, then, must be Amy Thiel. She certainly seemed to be well in command of the emergency, her manner assured and entirely unruffled.

I got out of the carriage, watching as another girl hurried out of the house. The new arrival made for a striking contrast to

Amy. Her dark-haired colouring was the exact opposite of Miss Thiel's fair complexion. She was small, and on the plump side, while Amy was willowy and fair. And her expression held all the worry and distress that Amy's lacked.

"Paul!" She reached to take the injured man's hand, and her voice, heavy with a broad Yorkshire accent, was also shaky with tears. "What's tha' done to thyself?"

"I'm all right." Paul Jeffries' face was white with pain, but he made an effort to smile. "Nothing wrong that can't be mended."

"Yes, Eliza, I'm sure he'll be all right," Amy said. She spoke more gently to the other girl than she had to the workmen. "Go along, you can sit with him and keep him company until the doctor arrives."

She stood back and watched as the workmen carried Paul's makeshift stretcher inside the house. Mrs. Thiel followed, with a murmur about asking Cook to prepare some tea and other refreshments for everyone.

Amy turned to me.

"You think this accident wasn't anything of the kind. Someone deliberately caused that ladder to break."

My eyebrows rose. Sabotage, of course, was precisely what the evidence seemed to prove. But it was unusual for an outsider to jump immediately to the same conclusion—especially since Amy hadn't seen the cuts made to the ladder's upper rungs.

"What makes you say that?"

Amy gestured impatiently. "I should have thought it obvious. You are an investigator, here with Mr. Holmes. Yet instead of going to join him on Powder Island, you came here with Paul. Therefore, you must have observed something about his fall to make you suspicious." She stopped, and now a line of worry did appear between her brows. "I'm afraid this will mean the opening of the new building at the factory will have to be delayed. As though people weren't already nervous enough! We'll be lucky if anyone is willing to come to a celebration dinner—much less come to work in the factory."

"The workers are uneasy, then?" I asked.

Amy shrugged her slim shoulders. "It's only to be expected, I suppose. After that sort of explosion—the entire building wasn't just damaged, it was obliterated. The workmen can't help thinking about what would have happened if they had been inside at the time—or if such a thing could happen again, despite all of my uncle's new safety measures." She sighed, then gave a slight shake of her head as though to throw off the moment's weariness, her eyes narrowing as she studied me. "I suppose you can't tell me what exactly about Paul's accident made you suspicious, since as far as you're concerned, I might be a suspect." She had a staccato, rapid-fire way of speaking, rather like the bullets fired from one of the machine guns her uncle's factory supplied with powder.

"I'm beginning to see why your mother described you as all practicality and business sense, Miss Thiel."

"Yes, poor mother." Amy's face turned wry. "She loves me, but she's also rather horrified by me. Just because I can't pretend to be a delicate, fainting, maidenly flower and never could. Please, come in," she added, leading the way through the still open front door.

Inside, Rexford Hall was decorated in the ornate style popular a half-century ago—and then only among the very wealthy: gilded furniture so ornate that it would have struck the Sun King himself as a trifle gaudy, walls papered in a rich blue brocade, and thick oriental rugs. Two large photographs hung on the heavy green wallpaper in the entry hall; one of them the Queen and Prince Albert, taken many years earlier, and one more recent, of the Prince of Wales at the helm of his yacht.

A tall mahogany coat rack stood to one side of the front door, with a white captain's cap and dark wool cape hanging from one of the hooks. The white cap was identical in style to the one worn by the Prince in the wall photograph.

I brushed by the cape as we passed. The hem was still a trifle damp.

"Those belong to Rex, my cousin," Amy said. "His room is upstairs, and of course, so is my uncle's."

"Is he here now?"

"I believe he's still at the factory. He was giving Mr. Holmes and Doctor Watson a tour. Probably stopped in here first for a dry cap and cape," Amy said. She led the way to the right of the front hall and into a small room that must, I thought, be the private office her mother had mentioned. It was far simpler in style than the rest of the house. The walls were painted a pale green. The furniture was well-crafted but plain: a wooden desk with papers tidily put away in individual dockets, a settee, a couple of chairs.

The window, looking out over the front drive, was covered only with a gauzy curtain that let in the winter's pale sunlight.

Amy seated herself behind the desk and motioned for me to sit.

"Now, what can I do to help your investigation? I've already spoken to Dr. Watson and Mr. Holmes."

"I'm sorry to make you go through it all again."

Amy waved that aside. "It's quite all right. The more times

one tells a story, the more likely it is for some forgotten or seemingly unimportant detail to come to light."

"That's quite true."

It was also unusual for an ordinary civilian to understand.

As though she'd heard my thought, Amy said, "Inspector Gregson told me so. When he was here to look into the explosion last spring."

"Yes, I spoke to him this morning about his investigation."

"You saw Tobias—I mean, Inspector Gregson?" Amy's voice altered, turning strained, somehow—as though she was trying to keep herself from sounding too eager. She toyed with a pen on the edge of her desk. "How is he?"

"He was demoted—he lost his rank of inspector and is now a constable in Whitechapel." I watched her as I spoke. "Apparently those in authority at Scotland Yard felt he had mishandled your case."

"But—" For the first time in our conversation, Amy looked as though she had been entirely shaken out of her briskly capable self-assurance. She stared at me, open-mouthed for what must have been a full five seconds before finally finding her voice. "But that is terrible! Worse than terrible—*criminal*!"

"You hadn't heard?"

It was difficult to believe that, as her uncle's secretary and assistant, Amy could have been unaware of Gregson's clash with Bradley Rexford. And yet her shock and outrage seemed genuine.

Amy shook her head. "No, I hadn't seen or spoken to him since … But how could anyone have faulted him? He only wanted to get to the truth!"

Twin bright spots of colour burned in her cheeks. One thing

at least I was certain of: if Bradley Rexford had exerted his influence to get Inspector Gregson demoted, Amy hadn't been a willing party to the campaign.

"Did you share Inspector Gregson's opinion that the explosion was no accident?" I asked.

Amy gestured impatiently. "Of course I did."

"Do you suspect anyone in particular?"

A shutter seemed to come down across Amy's face, the outrage dying, leaving her expression hard and self-contained once more.

"No. I do not know what or whom to believe—but I know the explosion was deliberate." She drew a ragged breath, then went on, her calm almost fully recovered now, "If you'd like me to tell you about the day of the explosion … to start with, my father went to the factory to make his usual Sunday morning inspection. I said goodbye to him that morning at breakfast, just as usual—never dreaming that in just a few short hours, nothing about my life would ever be the same, or that I would never see him again."

Her voice was flat and almost toneless, but her face was etched with an echo of raw pain that hadn't yet been smoothed out by time.

Either she was an unbelievably good actress, or she genuinely grieved her father's death.

"Was it customary for him to go alone?" I asked.

"Oh yes. Father liked to go when no one else was about, to be certain he could perform his inspections alone and uninterrupted. He would go in at sunrise and then stay till he had walked through all the dozen or so buildings. He had slowed down a bit in this past year or two—he had arthritis in one knee that made it painful for him to walk. But he still never missed a day of work or a single inspection."

A carriage that I assumed to be the doctor's was rolling up the drive and would probably interrupt us in another moment or two.

"Would you mind if I asked you an impertinent question?"

Amy's brows rose slightly, and then a humourless smile quirked the corners of her mouth. "You've been talking to Mother, so let me guess: does it have to do with my marrying Rex?"

"Not for the moment."

Amy looked surprised. "No?"

"No."

It was a truism of the art of detection that assembling evidence was like putting together the pieces of a jigsaw puzzle. One didn't get to choose the individual pieces—or to throw a piece out simply because it didn't appear at first glance to fit in with the others.

I couldn't for the moment entirely see how the woman who had approached Flynn with Bradley Rexford's watch fit in with the factory explosion. But it did fit, somehow—and what was more, I was beginning to have a glimmer of an idea that it was important.

As important as the man in the captain's cap and cape whom Flynn had followed.

"What I wanted to ask you was this: do you think it believable that your uncle should have visited a grog shop in the East End of London, where he made the acquaintance of a—shall we say, lady of the evening?"

"Oh." Amy's expression was momentarily blank.

I watched her. "That doesn't appear to surprise you nearly as much as it did your mother. She thought it entirely out of character."

Amy gave a harsh laugh. "Mother also thinks it incredibly kind of Uncle Bradley that he allows us to live at the Dower House—and continues to employ me."

Her voice was bitter.

"And you don't agree?"

It wasn't the doctor's carriage after all. The carriage drew to a halt in front of the steps, and Holmes sprang out.

A cold weight landed in the pit of my stomach. Amy was still speaking, but I was already out of the door and halfway to the entrance hall when Holmes burst in through the front door.

"Lucy!" It was seldom that I saw Holmes jarred out of his usual imperturbable calm, but his expression now was urgent. "Jack telephoned to the Powder Island Factory. We must return to London at once."

My heart lurched and then skittered to a sickening halt. If Jack had telephoned, it meant Jack was still alive. But something could have happened to Becky, or to Flynn—

"Gregson was attacked," Holmes said.

Amy gasped. "What?"

I turned to find her standing behind me, swaying a little, her face gone ashen to the lips.

Holmes nodded. "He was stabbed in the chest—on the street outside the Blue Bottle in Whitechapel. He is currently in hospital, and it is uncertain whether he will survive the night."

19. WATSON

The white-painted corridor of Saint Bartholomew's Hospital smelled strongly of harsh soap and carbolic acid. We sat in a row on an uncomfortable wooden bench: Holmes, Lucy, myself, and then Becky and Flynn.

Gregson had been taken into surgery, and there was now nothing for us to do but await the surgeon's news of whether his life had been saved.

"This is my fault," Lucy said. I had seldom heard her sound more distressed. "I went to see him this morning, to ask him about the Powder Island case. I don't know what exactly I told him, but something I said must have made him decide to resume his own line of investigation—something that led him to alarm the wrong person when they heard what he was doing. And this is the result."

Holmes seldom wasted what he would consider valuable brainpower on expressions of reassurance or sympathy. But his manner as he addressed Lucy was more gentle than usual.

"Any investigation carries with it its own regrets. So I will merely ask what you imagine Gregson himself would say if he could hear you."

Lucy drew a breath and gave Holmes a shaky half-smile. "He would probably say I shouldn't waste time feeling guilty when I could be accomplishing something useful, such as catching whoever stabbed him."

"Precisely. And to that end—" Holmes paused, leaning back on the bench and half closing his eyes. "You say, Becky, you first noticed Inspector Gregson at the cabstand?"

"Yes. At least, I think it was him. I never saw his face."

"He might easily have seen you and Flynn, though. In fact, I think we may assume that he did see the two of you." Holmes put the tips of his fingers together. "I would reconstruct Gregson's actions thus: he learned from Lucy that we believed Mr. Rexford to be threatened. Inquiries on Baker Street would have produced a witness who could have told him of the man in the captain's cap and black cape who apparently followed Mr. Bradley Rexford to Baker Street in a cab. His mind operating along similar lines to ours, Gregson looked for the cabbie."

"Then when he saw us, he must have decided to follow us, instead," Becky said. She looked as downcast as Lucy. "Maybe he thought we might get into trouble going to the Blue Bottle and wanted to keep watch. If that's true, it's also our fault he got hurt!"

"You did well to summon help as quickly as you did," Holmes said. "If Gregson survives, he will have you as well as the surgeons to thank. Also, you are forgetting the fruit vendor you saw. The one with the suspiciously new boots."

Becky looked up quickly. "You think he was following Gregson?"

"You saw no such person in the neighbourhood of the Blue Bottle?"

Becky screwed up her eyes in an effort of remembrance, but finally shook her head. "I don't think so. Flynn?"

Flynn shook his head.

"No matter." Holmes looked regretful, but resigned. "We

may take it this person changed clothing before continuing to follow Gregson—and caught up with him when he was waiting for you up the road from the gin shop."

"But who was it?" Becky asked.

"Ah. That is the question, is it not?" Holmes leaned back a little on the bench.

"We know it can't have been any of the suspects in the Powder Island case," Lucy said. "Or at least, not Amy or her mother, and not Bradley Rexford or his son, either. They were all in Twickenham at the time Gregson was attacked."

"We must assume Gregson contacted an outside party before he set out to track down the caped man—someone outside of the immediate Rexford family circle," Holmes said.

Lucy said, her voice quiet, "I told him the police files on Powder Island had disappeared."

She and Holmes exchanged a long look. The implication was, of course, clear even to me: only someone within either Scotland Yard or perhaps the Home Office would have had access to those files.

Holmes cleared his throat. "However, speculating as to the identity of that person is less likely to bear fruit than solving the problem of the explosion on Powder Island. Questioning Scotland Yard or the Home Office will at best earn us a number of doors slammed in our faces."

"And at worst alert our man to our investigation," Lucy finished.

"Indeed."

"So we're going to let whoever stabbed Gregson get away with it?" Becky asked. She sounded outraged.

"By no means." Holmes's face had a granite-hard, focused

look that I remembered well from past cases. No one seeing him now would think the malefactor who had sought to kill Gregson would escape unscathed. "I am merely stating that an indirect approach is likely in this case to suit us best. Once we have identified the person who set off the explosion on Powder Island, the other pieces of the puzzle will fall into place."

"And we may hope Gregson will recover and will himself be able to identify his attacker," I said.

The words seemed to echo hollowly in the sterile, empty hospital corridor, where each passing moment made it less and less likely that our hope would be realised.

A nurse in starched white cuffs and collar approached, and we all stiffened in anticipation of what news she might bring—but she hurried past without speaking and entered a patient's ward further down the hall.

I stopped myself from looking at my watch in an attempt to calculate what progress the surgeon might have made by now in his valiant efforts to repair the damage done by the unknown assailant's knife. Instead I said, "We have another conundrum, in that all of our key players are also alibied for the time of the explosion. Both Rexfords, father and son, were in church when the blast went off, as were Amy and her mother. There is, of course, Rexford's enemy, Mr. Jerrard."

I paused, glancing at Holmes, but his face remained impassive. Unless I was much mistaken, Holmes did not seem to think Mr. Jerrard a likely suspect, whatever he had told Rex. The very fact he had spoken of the possibility so freely to Rex would have told me as much.

"But any of the family could have rigged a detonator and timer," Lucy pointed out.

"True." Holmes's tone was musing. "There is also the possibility that the dead man himself was in some way responsible—that his death was the result of some accident or clumsiness in handling the explosives."

I looked at Holmes in surprise. "Do you seriously suspect Marcus Thiel?"

Holmes made a dismissive gesture. "Neither more nor less than I suspect anyone else at this juncture. But he had a better opportunity than anyone else to both plant and detonate the explosives, therefore he must remain on our list of possible suspects. He could have been bribed or threatened to set off the explosion."

"I suppose that's possible," Lucy said. "But it seems out of character for him. His wife and daughter aren't exactly impartial witnesses, of course. But I gained the impression from both of them that Marcus was a highly conscientious man. Amy said he had been troubled by arthritis in his knee these past two years, but he still never missed a single Sunday morning's—what is it?" she asked Holmes.

Holmes hadn't spoken, but he had made a small, sudden movement, as though struck by something she had said.

Holmes waved a hand. "Nothing at all. Please, go on."

Lucy frowned, but said, "For that matter, it's difficult to see what motive *any* of them could have had for sabotaging the factory. Who has benefited by the explosion, or the death of Marcus Thiel? Not Amy or her mother. They certainly didn't benefit financially. Amy has exactly the same job she did before, but they've lost Marcus's income as supervisor. Her mother implied it was only Rex's generosity that allowed them to stay at the Rexford Hall Dower House. And both are genuinely grieving for Marcus, I'm certain of that."

"Quite." Holmes's long fingers beat a restless tattoo on his trouser leg. "Bradley Rexford has been thrown into financial difficulties by the explosion. He is attempting to solve that with the incorporation. Meanwhile, his son Rex has been forced to go to work and give up his carefree life of yachting. According to his father, he has not been sailing since the explosion."

"He apparently hasn't retired his yachting apparel, though," Lucy said. "His cape and captain's cap were on the hall stand at Rexford Hall—and the hem of the cape was still damp."

"Ah." I caught a familiar gleam in Holmes's half-lidded gaze. "That is interesting. He was wearing a cape and captain's cap when he gave Watson and me a tour of the Rexford Works." He thought for a moment, and then said, "Flynn."

Flynn had been sliding further down on the bench, looking as though he were halfway to falling asleep, but he jerked upright at Holmes's mention of his name.

"Yes, sir?"

"Can you recall anything else about the girl who approached you with Mr. Rexford's watch?"

"I don't think so." Flynn rubbed the bridge of his nose. "Except for what I've already told you. She looked scared. She was out of breath when she first came up to me, and she said she didn't dare mention the name of the man who owned the watch …"

Holmes interrupted. "Her appearance, though. Was there any detail that struck you? Anything odd about her?"

"Well." Flynn considered. "I dunno if it's odd, but her clothes were all rumpled, just like I said before. And she'd got her face painted—but it was just smeared on anyhow, smudged all over her face, not just on her lips and cheeks."

"But that *is* something odd!" Becky sat up straighter. "A girl wouldn't bother to put on rouge and lip colour if she was going to do that bad a job of it. She would use a mirror—and even if she was too poor to afford one, she'd borrow one from a friend, or else use a shop window to see her reflection."

"Wait!" Flynn held up a hand. "I'd forgotten before, but something else was strange. I said the watch looked like a flash jerry, and she didn't know what I meant."

"Flash jerry being Cockney slang for an expensive pocket watch," Holmes said. He leaned forwards, definitely alert, now. "Can you repeat everything she said to you—her precise words—in as exact detail as you can?"

"I'll try." Flynn's brows knitted together. "She said she'd seen me talking to Mr. Holmes. And then she said, *I want you to do sommat for me.*"

Holmes held up a hand. "That will do."

Flynn looked at him, startled. "That's all?"

"Yes, that is quite enough confirmation."

"Confirmation," I repeated. "You know, then, who the guilty party is?"

"I would not go so far as to say that." Holmes looked at Lucy. "But we have narrowed the field down to two possibilities, each with roughly equal likelihood of being proved correct, would you say?"

Lucy pursed her lips, considering. "I might put the split around sixty-forty."

Holmes gestured to Flynn and Becky. "I have an assignment for the two of you," he said. "Tomorrow I want you to go to Rexford Hall."

Flynn and Becky listened thoughtfully as he spoke further,

quietly, out of my hearing, and then nodded.

I sighed. "I assume when all of this is over, I will discover what all of you are talking about. But for the moment—"

I broke off as a white-coated doctor approached our bench, his expression tired and grave.

"Mr. Holmes?"

"Yes?" Holmes's tone was sharp.

The doctor cleared his throat. "I'm happy to tell you it looks as though Constable Gregson will pull through. It was touch and go—and of course we must hope that he avoids infection—but I believe I may say he is for the moment out of danger."

"Ah." Holmes released a long breath. "Thank you, doctor." He remained motionless a moment, then stood up with renewed energy and made to stride off.

"Where are you going?" I asked.

"This news accords quite well with our plans." Holmes spoke over his shoulder. "I intend to find a telephone and tell those at Rexford Hall that Gregson is still unconscious, but expected to make a full recovery."

20. LUCY

I positioned myself near the massive stone gate of St. Bartholomew's Hospital, looking out upon the stone-paved, noisy neighbourhood of the London Central Meat Market. A statue of Henry VIII crowned the stone archway—an unlikely figure, I would have said, to offer hope or reassurance to the sick. But the street outside the gate was crowded, even at night, with a steady stream of the ill and injured seeking relief. The uniformed porter was busy with mothers holding sick and crying babies, men with their arms done up in makeshift bandages or slings, and one old woman begging to have a rotten tooth extracted.

I waited in the deepest part of the shadows, pinching myself to keep awake as the clock of a nearby church tower chimed first one o'clock in the morning, then half past the hour, and then two. I ought to have been too on-edge to be tired, given that it was an attempted murder we were expecting—*another* attempted murder, meant to remedy the first effort's having failed.

But it had been a long day, and the cold and the darkness—and the constant parade of human suffering and frailty before me—were making it hard to stay focused.

Becky and Flynn had long since gone back to Baker Street to sleep out the remainder of the night, so as to be fresh for the next day's assignment Holmes had given them. Holmes and Watson were still here. But the Western Gate was far from the only entrance to the huge hospital building, and we needed to take every precaution that none of our suspects slipped in and caught us unaware.

The porter escorted an old man in, directing him to the out-patients' ward to the left of the gate.

I watched him totter off, clutching his own brown glass bottle in which to carry home any medicines he was prescribed. Then I stiffened.

The porter's back was still turned to the outside gate as he, too, watched the old man make his unsteady way across the cobblestones. And while the gate was momentarily unattended, a tall, slim figure slipped inside, briefly joined a group of mothers who were sitting on the steps of another ward, waiting for the matron of the infants' department to arrive—and then stood up and made for a door leading into the hospital's main floor.

As the figure moved, a beam of light from a gas lantern in the courtyard fell on it, showing fair hair and a young woman's pale, nervous face.

My heart dropped. I had agreed with Holmes that there was a forty percent likelihood of this outcome. But I was still sorry.

I hadn't wanted it to be Amy Thiel for whom I was waiting.

I straightened, stepping quickly out from the shadows and following Amy into the hospital. I stopped at the end of the corridor, where the hallway opened out into a reception lobby, with a matron on duty behind a central desk.

There were more people about here—patients and doctors and nurses hurrying to and fro. But I heard the heavyset and stern-looking matron telling Amy in a clipped tone that visiting hours were over for the day and would not commence again until nine o'clock tomorrow morning.

"I understand." Amy's voice, higher than usual, and sounding frightened, reached me. "But if you could just tell me what room Constable Gregson is in? Please? Then I could come back and see him tomorrow. He is—that is, he is a very close friend of my family."

My eyebrows edged upwards. It was one of Holmes's maxims that a murderer always made at least one mistake—but it was seldom so great a blunder as openly inquiring as to the location of their proposed victim.

I missed hearing the matron's reply, but she must have been more soft-hearted than she first appeared, because Amy stepped back from the desk with a look of quick relief and a heartfelt, "Thank you! Oh—thank you!"

She turned away, walking slowly towards an outer door, but then, as soon as the matron began to attend to another patient, she reversed direction, heading quickly towards a door marked *Recovery Wards*.

I slipped my hand into my pocket, making sure I had ready access to the revolver I carried there, and followed.

21. WATSON

The door to Gregson's hospital room opened and I heard stealthy footsteps approach the bed.

I was there at Holmes's direction. Gregson lay quiet, still unconscious from his surgery. I had stationed myself behind a fabric hospital screen, hidden from view.

Now, looking around the edge of the screen, I saw someone in a captain's cap and a long cape, standing beside the bed, and a pair of hands holding a pillow. The attacker was reaching towards Gregson, about to smother him.

I sprang from my chair. A moment more, and I had clapped my hand onto the attacker's wrist.

I saw my adversary, his face twisted in surprise and rage. *Young Rex Rexford.*

My own fury surged. I thought nothing of tactics or how I might be disadvantaged by my greater age. My thoughts were focused solely on protecting Gregson from this would-be murderer. I tackled him, but he stayed erect. He tried to twist out of my grip, but I clung to him. I saw a pistol in his belt, beneath his cape. Locked in our struggle, we stumbled into the hospital hallway. I bore down on him, throwing him to the tiles of the hallway floor, and I heard a woman's voice.

"Rex!" It was the voice of Amy Thiel. "What are you doing here?"

"He was about to kill Gregson," I said.

Rex said nothing. His hand scrabbled for his pistol.

"Drop it," came Lucy's voice, hard and cold. She had her Ladysmith drawn, and she pressed the muzzle into Rex's cheek, just below his eye. "Now, do I have your attention? You can simply nod. I don't want any more noise to disturb Inspector Gregson."

I peeled back Rex's cape and took away his pistol. Lucy kept her Ladysmith aimed at Rex as I removed his belt and used it to bind his wrists behind his back.

"Now," said Lucy, "I suggest we all go peacefully to the visitors' waiting room. It is empty, and we can speak there without creating more disturbance."

We sat on the wooden benches in the waiting room. Rex kept his eyes down, unable to meet the questioning gaze of Amy. He said nothing.

A few moments later, Sherlock Holmes arrived, along with two constables.

"We have the papers from the sale of your yacht, Mr. Rexford," Holmes said. "Courtesy of the Registry of Ships."

"What of it?"

"The papers reveal your true purpose for selling."

"I was raising capital for our family company. Everyone knows that."

Holmes cut him off. "You were acquiring a murder weapon, in a way you thought would not be traced to you. But in your usual careless fashion, you failed to read the paperwork for the conveyance of the yacht, and by so failing, you have betrayed yourself. Do you care to explain how you engineered the explosion?"

Rex sat mute, lips compressed, eyes staring blankly.

"Very well. The evidence we have is enough to arrest you. The constables will soon take you to the Old Bailey for your arraignment. Do not hope for bail, for it will not be granted, considering you were just now caught in the act of attempting the murder of a Metropolitan Police officer."

Rex remained mute.

Amy Thiel said, "I truly don't understand, Mr. Holmes. Can you please explain what the papers connected to the sale of Rex's yacht have to do with the explosion?"

"The papers called for the vessel to be sold in 'voyage-ready' condition. It was not. One important piece of equipment, required by government and insurance safety regulations, was missing. The papers record that the seller of the yacht gave a credit to the buyer in the purchase price in order to compensate, and that the buyer assumed all liability resulting from the lack of the missing component."

Young Rex's lip curled in a sneer. "Just what component was missing?"

"The papers make it quite plain. The missing component was the safety flare gun, otherwise known as a Very pistol, required for emergencies to call for help."

"Trivial," Rex said. "I can't be bothered with those details. I just signed the papers that they put in front of me. If there was something missing from my yacht, this is the first I've heard of it."

"You set off the explosion with that flare gun. You used a tripwire."

"I deny it," Rex said. "Nothing of the kind was found at the site."

"But you and your father were the first on the scene after the explosion, and your father recalls you running ahead. You hid the wire and flare gun and then returned to dispose of them later."

"You cannot prove it, Mr. Holmes."

"When we spoke at the top of the shot tower, I noticed how pleased you were when I suggested that Jerrard had rowed to the building and lit the fuse to a bomb. In fact it was you, Rex, not Jerrard, who rowed there. You came to the building at night, when no one could see you. You connected a tripwire to the cocked trigger of the flare gun from your yacht. Then you rowed back to the Rexford Hall dock and crept to bed. The next morning, you went to church with your father. Then when the parties were all in church, each with an alibi, the explosion occurred."

"I don't understand," said Amy.

"Rex's goal was not merely to destroy the glazing works building. He wanted to kill your father."

"No!" Rex cried.

Amy turned to Rex, her eyes brimming with tears. "Why would you do such a thing?"

For the first time, Rex's air of confidence seemed to desert him. He lowered his gaze and sat silent.

Holmes said, "Miss Thiel, Rex had a financial motive, and perhaps another. Your father had begun to support the other workers in their demands for better wages. With him out of the way, factory wages could be kept low and profits maximized. Isn't that correct, Rex? Or did you have a second reason? Did you somehow imagine that the loss of her father would make Miss Thiel more vulnerable, and thus more susceptible to an offer of marriage from you?"

Rex stared at the floor.

Amy's face was horror-stricken.

"The only way to be certain that Marcus Thiel was present when the building exploded was to have him *cause* the explosion. And, knowing that Marcus dragged his feet when he walked, due to his arthritic knee, Rex used a tripwire. When Marcus shuffled into the glazing building, hitting the tripwire, the flare gun fired, and the burning flare ignited the gunpowder."

Amy's voice was raw and ragged. "Rex. Tell me it's not true. Tell me Mr. Holmes is wrong."

Rex took a deep breath, and somehow his air of confidence seemed to return. "Not to worry. No one's going to prove it. My father will get me a top-shelf barrister."

Amy stared at Rex for a long moment. Then she turned her back on him.

After a nod to the two constables from Holmes, Rex was taken away.

"Will he get away with it, Mr. Holmes?" asked Amy. "Will he really walk free after killing my father?"

Holmes's face was grim. "We have Dr. Watson's testimony to support a charge of assault on Constable Gregson here at the hospital, and perhaps attempted murder. That will be enough to hold him temporarily. But if Rex is to be convicted for your father's murder, my deductive reasoning, accurate though it may be, will not be enough. We will need hard, convincing evidence, and in sufficient quantity to convince a jury."

22. WATSON

Outside Gregson's hospital room the street was dark, barely illuminated by a few gas lamps. I stood by his window for a moment, my thoughts swirling. What would Holmes do to find the evidence we needed? And how would we protect Gregson from those who were trying to silence him? Young Rex had been caught, but who else was out there in the darkness? I thought of the flare-gun young Rex had used. I thought of the murderous air-gun used by Colonel Moran.

I closed the curtain.

In his bed, the unconscious Gregson continued to breathe peacefully, still under the influence of the sedative he had received.

Holmes turned to Amy. "I still have two questions, Miss Thiel. First, why did you follow Bradley Rexford in the guise of his son? And second, why did you pretend to be a cockney woman from the Blue Bottle who wished to return your uncle's purloined watch?"

Amy opened and closed her mouth, but no sound emerged.

"You were the passenger in the cab, Miss Thiel, wearing the cape and the captain's hat." Holmes said. "Only someone who knew your uncle had made an appointment to see me in my Baker Street rooms could have arrived there first. And only someone connected with your family would have chosen the conspicuous captain's cap and cape. You knew, because you had arranged the appointment. And you had access to Rex's wardrobe, since you had your own office in Rexford Hall, where he lived. From your choice of disguise, you expected to be seen by your uncle, and to be incorrectly identified as his son. Am I correct thus far?"

"I—" Amy still seemed unable to speak.

It was Lucy who appeared to take pity on her. "You knew, didn't you," she said quietly. "You knew it was Rex who had caused the factory explosion."

"I didn't *know*." Amy flung out her hands in a gesture of appeal. "I suspected. But I hadn't a shred of proof to confirm my suspicions. My uncle would never have believed me—his own son? Guilty of sabotage and murder? I could scarcely believe it—I didn't *want* to believe it. I had known Rex ever since we were children! And yet I also knew how little obstacles mattered to him, when it was a matter of getting his own way." She stopped, biting her lip. "I thought if I disguised myself as Rex and followed my uncle to Baker Street, he might see him, lose confidence in Rex, at least a little, and make him more likely to believe anything Mr. Holmes uncovered to discredit him."

"And the purloined watch?" Holmes asked.

Amy lowered her head. "That is the action of which I am least proud," she said. "But I wanted to stop the incorporation my uncle was planning! I knew a board of directors would never permit me to keep my position—a young woman in a position of authority at a gunpowder factory? They would die of horror at the very notion. So, I thought that if I could cast a shadow on my uncle's character, perhaps it would be enough to make the underwriters not want to go through with the incorporation."

"Was that the only reason you wanted to prevent it—so you could keep your job?"

Amy sat up straighter. "Not just that. Part of my job was to correspond with the insurance company. We had insurance coverage that included more than enough to rebuild. We had a 'lost profits' clause that should have provided enough money to pay wages to keep the factory running. So, most employees should have been able to continue work."

"So you think funds from incorporation weren't needed?"

Amy sighed. "Yes, I'm sure there was something wrong. At any rate, I thought that my uncle having his watch supposedly stolen by a lady of the night from the Blue Bottle, a notorious late-night haunt for disreputable men and women ... well, it would surely be enough to besmirch his reputation."

"You were not very convincing as a cockney barmaid," Holmes said.

She nodded. "I was afraid you would see through me. When I saw you talking to that street boy on your doorstep, I panicked. I told the cabman to drive off. But then I saw the street boy following and thought he might be taken in more easily. So I stopped the cab at the railway station and made sure the street boy had seen me. In the station I stuffed the captain's cap and cape into my canvas holdall, put on my lip rouge, and hurried back to 221B."

"Where you waited for Flynn and told your tale of the stolen watch," Holmes said.

"Which wasn't a crime," Lucy said.

"I am sorry for it, though. I believe—" Amy gave a shake of her head and exhaled a shaky breath. "I believe I have been almost unbalanced with grief for my father these past months. Perhaps the more so because I could not admit my suspicions of Rex to myself. How could I have been foolish enough to work for a man like him all these months?"

"You didn't know," Lucy said.

Amy's eyes moved to Gregson's pale, still figure on the bed. "You will—" she swallowed. "Will you please let me know how he fares?"

Again, it was Lucy who answered her. "Yes, of course we will."

Amy bowed her head. "Then I must return to my mother and my uncle. The news of Rex's arrest will devastate them."

We watched her depart, her face pale but her posture brave, square-shouldered and erect.

Holmes was the first to break the silence. "Watson, I propose we should take the rest of the night by Gregson's bedside in shifts. Would you prefer to remain on guard first, or shall I?"

"Guard?" I repeated in blank surprise.

Holmes's expression was grimly set, his voice determined. "I think this matter is very far from being over and done. And we have a great deal of work to do."

23. LUCY

St. Andrews Church was filled with celebrants for the opening of the new building. The mood of the gathering felt cautiously optimistic. I hadn't spoken to Mr. Rexford personally, but according to Holmes, he had taken the news of his son's guilt more calmly than might have been expected, being more concerned with proving his innocence and keeping the case out of the newspapers. Perhaps as a parent he had fewer illusions than anyone about the strength of Rex's character.

Nor, it would appear, had the factory workers and their families been overly fond of Bradley Rexford, Junior, or overly grieved that he would no longer be their supervisor. There was, it seemed to me, *a good-riddance-to-bad-rubbish* attitude towards Rex's arrest, and a feeling that perhaps now the celebration tonight could truly mark a fresh start.

Jack and I, though, were standing outside the church in the freezing cold—and I was beginning to wonder why.

"I don't suppose Holmes told you what we're supposed to be looking for?" I asked.

"Anything suspicious or out of the ordinary was as much as he'd tell me," Jack said.

"We're looking for a needle in a sea of other needles, in other words."

"Your father's obviously expecting trouble," Jack said.

So was I, if I was honest. My skin was crawling with a nameless, uneasy sensation that had nothing to do with the chill weather.

"The man who walked in a few minutes ago—tall, heavyset, with a green checked waistcoat and a red handkerchief in his pocket," I said. "What colour boots was he wearing?"

"Brown," Jack said without even a pause for thought. "The lace on the left foot was fraying. Why? You think that's important?"

"Not really. I just wanted to see whether I could trip you up as to any of the details."

"Is that a challenge?"

A few latecomers from the village were still trickling in, and his eyes tracked them, taking in, I was certain, every detail of their appearances, from the tarnished belt buckle on one man to the colour of the feather in a stout woman's hat.

"Maybe."

Jack grinned. "What stakes are we playing for?"

If I were Becky, I'd ask for the privilege of picking desserts for a week. "If I win, you tell me as much as you can about Sergeant O'Hara?"

A shadow crossed Jack's gaze. "I'd do that anyway. Lucy—"

"It's all right," I interrupted him. "What we really ought to do for now is split up and make a circuit of the church. This is the main entrance, but there are others. All were locked on Holmes's orders, but we should make certain of that—and that everything else is as it should be—before the speech-making starts."

Jack nodded. "All right. North or south?"

"I'll take north." That would make my route include a circuit around the banquet hall. "We can meet in the middle."

Jack turned and started around the southern side of Saint Andrews. I watched him go, trying to identify where the cold, crawling sense of some looming disaster was coming from. It wasn't just Holmes's warning—

I stopped as I caught sight of a familiar figure in a blue police uniform approaching the church, then disappearing around the side of the banquet hall.

Gregson.

His presence here wasn't suspicious, per se, but it was unexpected. Holmes had arranged for an official police guard to be placed in Gregson's hospital room after he and Watson had completed their night vigil. Jack had been getting updates from the doctors about Gregson's condition, so I knew he was recovering well and ready to be discharged.

What had brought him here, though?

Frowning, I started after him.

Then I saw the answer.

Gregson and Amy were standing close together in the small, sheltered alcove of the church's south porch. Gregson was speaking, his voice rough and husky. I caught only the final words.

"—insane. You deserve so much better. What would your mother—or your uncle—say about you marrying a common police constable?"

Gregson broke off. He had just caught sight of Jack, coming around the church from the other side.

"Sergeant Kelly."

To judge by his expression, Jack had heard as much of Gregson's words as I had done, but he said only, "Good to see you up and about again, sir."

Gregson's face jerked, as with a quick flash of pain. "No need to call me *sir* anymore. You outrank me these days."

"Maybe not. Sir," Jack said. His eyes met mine in silent

question over the top of Gregson's head, and I nodded. "But I'd still be glad of your thoughts on the security measures in place for the event this afternoon," Jack finished. "We haven't got enough manpower to vet all the late arrivals."

"I—yes, of course." Gregson went to join him, and they moved off together, towards a handsome black carriage just rolling up to the front of the church.

Amy lifted her head and saw me. Her expression quivered, and for a moment, it seemed likely she would simply bolt past me without a word. But then she lifted her head.

"I suppose you heard that." She didn't phrase it as a question, nor did she give me time to answer. Her cheeks were flushed, her eyes over-bright and glittering with unshed tears. "Are you going to tell me I'm insane, as well?"

"For wanting to marry a policeman? Hardly. That was my husband who just went off with Constable Gregson. You didn't know?"

"Your—" Amy stared. "Oh. No, I didn't know." She looked past me towards Jack and Gregson, her expression softening a little. "It was good of him, not to make Tobias feel inferior because he's lost his rank of inspector."

"Jack *is* good." I paused, then added, "And not that your choice of a husband is any of my business, but he also tried to give me much the same speech Gregson was giving you just now—about how I deserved better than to be married to a low-ranking police constable. He was only a constable when we got engaged."

"And what did you say?"

"That I'd somehow missed the vote where he was put in charge of deciding what was best for me."

Amy gave me a small, fractured twist of a smile. "I wish I could hope that would work as well on Tobias. He—" She stopped, frowning as she apparently caught sight of something behind me. "Why, that's Mr. Jerrard's carriage pulling up. What on earth is he doing here?" Her frown deepened. "He and my uncle loathe one another. If my uncle catches sight of him—"

Jerrard, a heavy, florid-looking man in a black top hat and fur-trimmed overcoat, was just descending from the newly arrived black carriage. His lips were pursed, his nostrils pinched as though all the world had a faintly rancid smell. Or maybe he was just indignant because his carriage driver hadn't come round to put down the set of steps so he could climb down from the carriage with ease.

The coachman was muffled in several layers of scarves that covered the lower half of his face, and had a hat pulled down low over his eyes. His brown boots appeared new. Instead of attending to his passenger, he seemed to be fumbling with something placed in the box under his seat.

I saw what he'd picked up. Just a fraction of a second later he stood tall, pistol in hand.

"Jack!"

My scream caught Jack's attention, and he looked in a flash from me to the carriage. Gregson, too, caught sight of the gun, and he and Jack both broke into a run towards the coachman.

But Mr. Rexford had come out of the church—and he, too, was armed.

"For God's sakes, what do you think you're doing?" he shouted at the coachman. "Drop your weapon or I'll fire!"

The rest seemed to happen in a blur that left me unable to tell who had fired first, the coachman or Mr. Rexford. But the sharp crack of a gunshot rent the air—

And then, a bare split-second later, the carriage exploded in a deafening roar and a flash of yellow-orange flames.

24. WATSON

We were at the rear of the St. Andrews church sanctuary, just within the sheltered area beneath the south alcove. I was treating Gregson and Jack for the minor burns and cuts they had sustained from the blast. All I had available was cold water and a towel from the church kitchen.

I had every confidence that both men would make a full recovery from their surface wounds. However, I was keeping a close eye on Gregson. Already weakened from being stabbed yesterday, he had now been knocked unconscious and had possibly sustained a concussion.

We had carried him away from the explosion site. Getting him into a seated position, I thought, would accelerate his return to consciousness and also give me a better opportunity to assess his condition.

Now both he and Jack were side by side, in the rear pew. Jack, fully alert, was with me watching Gregson. Both of us were waiting impatiently for signs of wakefulness.

After several minutes had elapsed, Gregson's eyes flickered. His head came upright. "What happened?" he asked.

"Mr. Jerrard and his coachman were both killed," I said.

Gregson closed his eyes for a moment. Then he asked, "Amy?"

"She's gone with Lucy to fetch some proper dressings for your injuries: burn ointment and gauze," I said. "Don't make any sudden movements. Just stay calm and rest for a bit. Jack is here beside you."

"Where is Holmes?"

"He's outside, examining the site of the explosion. Mr. Rexford is with him."

A few moments later, Lucy and Amy arrived. Each insisted on ministering the burn ointment directly to her respective man. I encouraged this, knowing the medical risk in their misapplying the ointment was far outweighed by the strong emotional reward. For a patient to have a loved one care for him is often the best aid to healing.

Holmes returned, with Mr. Rexford close behind him. He took in the scene at once, and I thought I saw a momentary smile of satisfaction as he nodded towards Lucy and Jack.

Rexford's eyes were on Holmes. It was apparent that Holmes had not yet shared his conclusions.

Then Holmes spoke. "The carriage was packed with sticks of dynamite. One of the bullets fired must have struck the dynamite, causing the shock that set off the explosion."

Mr. Rexford shook his head wonderingly. "I suppose Jerrard must have planned to drive his carriage up to the church and detonate it as an act of sabotage."

"Someone certainly planned for tonight's explosion," Holmes said.

The odd note in Holmes's tone must have struck Mr. Rexford, as well, because his brows lowered. "What do you mean, Mr. Holmes?"

"I mean, Mr. Rexford, that I have seldom met a man with his hand in so many tills at the same time."

Mr. Rexford drew himself up. "I find your tone offensive."

"Then you will find the facts I am about to state still less to your liking. You and Mr. Jerrard have maintained the appearance of being rivals and enemies in public. But in private, the two of you were working closely together."

"Ridiculous!"

"So closely, in fact, you were even willing to make your own son into a murderer in order to uphold your end of the bargain."

Mr. Rexford's jaw dropped open, and a dull, brick-red colour began to suffuse his cheeks.

"Are you suggesting—"

"I am more than suggesting, Mr. Rexford." Holmes's voice had the crisp, cold snap of a whip. "I am telling you. I do not imagine for a single moment that the idea of blowing up the factory and incidentally murdering Marcus Thiel came into your son's mind without assistance. His admiration for you made him easy to manipulate. You must have worked on him gradually—hinting to him that if something were to happen to Marcus, he would be eligible to step into the position of factory supervisor, and how you had every confidence he would do well in that regard. You likely spoke approvingly of a marriage with Amy, and of the dynasty such a marriage would create. We saw the photograph of the Queen and her cousin, Prince Albert, in your front hallway, as well as another photograph of the Prince of Wales, at the helm of the Royal Yacht. The marriage with Amy would emulate the Royal intrafamily connection."

"Those photographs are evidence of my son's patriotism and family loyalty. As far removed from evidence of a crime as they could possibly be."

"Your son is indeed loyal. Even though not denying his guilt, he refused to incriminate you. Did you suggest how easily an explosion might be touched off by a flare gun, and how the explosion would put many of the employees out of work and make them appreciate the wages they had once been paid? No more attempts to organise a trade union to demand better working conditions. The workers would be grateful to return to their jobs and would no longer ask for higher pay. The business would grow and prosper and might one day sustain the full-size racing yacht your son yearned for. And you told him the insurance proceeds would cover the costs of rebuilding."

Mr. Rexford seemed to make an effort to speak, but no sound emerged.

"Then, in keeping with your policy for never treating honestly with anyone, you also pocketed the insurance payment after the explosion," Holmes went on. "And all the while you pretended that the factory was in dire financial straits and needed you to take out a loan, and to bring in capital through incorporation."

Rexford finally found his voice. "Completely untrue!"

"The 'loan' was really a bribe from Jerrard to sabotage your own business and temporarily close down most of the factory. When the new building was complete, and your employees were eager to get back to work, you and Mr. Jerrard could have played out another pretty little comedy like the one you enacted for Watson's and my benefit, pretending once more to be mortal enemies. Mr. Jerrard expected to further that performance when he arrived here today. Then the two of you come to a business settlement, the corporate underwriters would take over, and you both would split the proceeds of the incorporation."

"Mr. Holmes, you are completely deranged."

"But you needed the support of the underwriters. So you brought me in to investigate the first investigation to impress them with your zeal to uncover the truth. To induce me to take the case, you sent yourself the anonymous letter made with newspaper clippings. Of course, you thought your crimes were too well concealed for me to uncover."

"You haven't uncovered anything. You are only speculating."

"We shall see about that," Holmes replied calmly. "You had also paid or bribed one of your own employees, first, to follow Gregson and kill him, and when that did not succeed, to take the place of Mr. Jerrard's coachman. He bought new boots with some of your money. You also gave him a gun—an empty one, no doubt—and instructed him to wave it around and make a show of frightening Mr. Jerrard. He, unfortunate soul, thought along with everyone else that Mr. Jerrard was an enemy trying to destroy his livelihood. He did not know you had arranged for dynamite to be loaded into Mr. Jerrard's carriage. Nor did he know that you, using the coachman's weapon as an excuse, would fire your own revolver into the carriage, detonating the explosion. You planned to keep both Mr. Jerrard's bribe money, what remained of the insurance payout after the building had been replaced, and, later, the proceeds of the incorporation, without anyone being the wiser." Holmes stopped and regarded Mr. Rexford with a cold, steel-hard gaze. "But now you will need to spend much of your money to organise legal defence teams for both yourself and your son."

"I admit nothing," said Rexford. "And you have no evidence."

Amy, her face aghast, stood up and strode forwards to come face to face with her uncle. "You are as evil as your son," she said. "I am ashamed to have wasted so many years working for you."

To my surprise, Rexford pushed her away with a violent shove.

She staggered back and collided with me.

Then he whirled and ran for his carriage.

I started to run after him, but Holmes put a restraining hand on my arm.

"Give him a minute," he said, "and then he may lead us to evidence."

"I'm with you," Jack said.

25. FLYNN

While everyone was away at the celebration, Flynn and Becky had broken into Rexford Hall, acting on Mr. Holmes's instructions. They were ransacking the place for clues.

But they hadn't found anything so far, and now they heard a carriage rattling up the driveway.

On the ground floor, they'd found a white canvas holdall in the closet of a small office. On the upper floor, they'd found some business papers in Mr. Rexford's desk. Flynn stuffed those in the holdall. The dustbin was empty, which was a disappointment, for Mr. Holmes had asked particularly that they check the dustbins and retrieve everything, especially old newspapers.

They'd moved into the bedroom and office suite at the other end of the hall, where young Mr. Rexford had lived until he'd been taken off to jail. They were searching Rex's room when they heard the clatter of wheels and hoofbeats and saw a big, bearded man in the coach-box, lashing furiously at the horses, coming closer to the house.

"We've got to get out!" Becky said, looking down from the window. "He's almost here!"

Flynn said. "In a minute." The dustbin in this room was also empty. But there was a neat stack of newspaper-looking magazines on the bookshelf. Neat, that is, except one in the middle, the spine of which bulged out oddly from the edge of the stack. Flynn examined it, and found that the entire contents had been removed. Only the magazine cover remained. It showed a picture of an enormous sailing vessel, and the name on the cover was *Yachting World*.

They could hear Mr. Rexford stomping up the front porch stairs and opening the door.

Flynn had an idea.

"Take the back stairs to the kitchen. Hurry!"

"Why?"

"Because up here the maid emptied the dustbins. But maybe she hasn't finished burning the trash downstairs."

Mr. Rexford's boots clumped up the carpeted front steps. Flynn and Becky eased themselves down the back stairs, practically sliding, leaning onto the railing and taking as much weight off their feet as they could.

They crept into the kitchen. There were two dustbins, one large, by the fireplace and the other, the smaller one, by the back door.

The large dustbin was full of papers.

"Quiet," said Flynn. They'd forgotten to close the door to the back stairs, and they could hear Mr. Rexford going from room to room, slamming one door after the other.

Which meant Mr. Rexford could hear them.

Becky held the canvas holdall open while Flynn stuffed in the papers. Some food wrappers. Some envelopes and catalogues. The day's newspaper. Yesterday's newspaper.

And a group of smaller pages, magazine-size newsprint, with *Yachting World* printed across the top of each.

Flynn riffed through the pages. He held up one.

There were two rectangular holes in that page, where two words had been cut out.

Becky's eyes lit up. Flynn stuffed the magazine pages on top of everything else in the holdall. But as he turned to go, the holdall swung out and knocked a metal pitcher off the big centre kitchen table. Becky and Flynn froze at the racket as the pitcher clanged and clattered on the hard tile floor.

A roar came from upstairs, and then came the sound of heavy footfalls pounding down the steps.

Flynn grabbed the holdall and mimed the word, "Run!"

On the way out, he carefully knocked over the other dustbin, the one with the food waste, spilling the foul-smelling contents onto the porch steps.

Then he and Becky ran, trying not to slip on the snowy path, until they reached the garden.

Hiding for a moment behind a tall hedge, they saw Mr. Rexford stumble out of the kitchen and fall onto the back porch. He hauled himself up, his face florid, trying to wipe the putrid garbage from his hands, his head turning right and left as he scanned the property.

Flynn gave a smile of satisfaction as he saw the big man's trouser legs were soaked through at the knees.

Then he saw Rexford pull a pistol from his pocket.

Flynn picked up a rock and hurled it as far as he could, to the woodpile at the right side of the building. It landed with a clatter.

Mr. Rexford took a few cautious steps in the direction of the sound.

Flynn and Becky took off running in the opposite direction. From behind them they heard Mr. Rexford, bellowing, "I see you! Come back or I'll shoot!"

They ran to the front of the Hall.

And saw a police carriage racing up the drive, the driver lashing at the horses.

The driver was Mr. Holmes. Beside him on the driver's box was Jack, holding a shotgun.

From behind them a shot rang out.

"He's got a pistol!" Flynn yelled, pulling Becky down with him alongside the road.

Jack raised the shotgun to his shoulder. "Drop it, Rexford!" he shouted. "Hands up!"

They heard the pistol hit the gravel driveway.

Flynn and Becky stood aside as the police carriage drove past. A moment later, both Mr. Holmes and Jack had leaped from the carriage. Jack hauled Mr. Rexford around and was locking handcuffs onto his wrists.

Becky waited while Flynn gave Mr. Holmes the canvas holdall.

"We've got it, Mr. Holmes," she said.

Mr. Holmes said, "Well done."

He gave each of them a pat on the shoulder.

26. LUCY

I approached the door of flat 221A Baker Street, then stopped at the sound of voices from inside.

"Stabbed and blown up in the self-same week." Gregson's voice was weak, raspy with fatigue.

"Ought to set some kind of record with the Force," Jack agreed.

On Holmes's insistence, we had brought Gregson—still drifting in and out of consciousness—back to Baker Street to recover from the effects of the bombing. We had been taking it in turns to sit with him, and I had been about to spell Jack so he could return to Scotland Yard.

"I need to get up—get out of here," Gregson's voice came from behind the door panel.

"Oh? Why's that?"

I seemed to be making a habit today of eavesdropping on Gregson's private conversations, but his next words kept me rooted in place outside the door.

"The same reason I can't have anything to do with Amy. Because I'm a danger to anyone who gets too close to me." Gregson drew a ragged breath, then said, his voice so low I could just barely make it out. "The Syndicate's behind this. And if you don't know what that means—" he broke off, and I pictured him searching Jack's expression. "You do know. Don't you."

"I know."

I almost shivered at the tone of Jack's voice. I had never heard him sound quite so grim.

"Then you'll have heard what happens to anyone who sets himself against them."

"Yeah. I know that, too. But I also know there's no place safer in London for you than this room right here—and that the shape you're in, you might as well sign your own death certificate if you try to walk out now."

"But—"

"Get some rest," Jack said. "We'll talk more about this later."

Gregson must have felt even worse and weaker than I imagined, because he didn't argue, only fell silent. A moment later, Jack appeared in the doorway.

He didn't look at all surprised to see me. He'd probably heard my footsteps on the stairs.

"The Syndicate?" I asked.

Jack ran a hand across his face. "Crime. Highly organised crime. Not just your run-of-the-mill street gang kind. They've got members everywhere—a whole network of bribery and corruption that runs straight up to the highest levels."

"Including the police force and the Home Office, obviously." I was oddly surprised at how calm and quiet my voice sounded. Cold was burrowing into me, but my words came out flat. "If someone either at Scotland Yard or the Home Office was being paid to squash the investigation into Powder Island … can we take it that either Mr. Rexford or his late associate Mr. Jerrard—or both—were Syndicate men?"

Jack gave me a wary look. He was probably surprised at how calm I sounded, too.

"Jerrard's the more likely candidate, I'd say, from the look of those papers Becky and Flynn found. Rexford's trying to move up in the world, but he's not rich enough or influential enough for the Syndicate to bother with him."

I nodded. "How long have you known about them? Wait—no. It would have to be since your training days, wouldn't it? Since you knew Sergeant O'Hara when you were going through police training together."

"Yes."

"And Sergeant O'Hara somehow tried to fight back against the Syndicate, and they killed him for it? That's what's been troubling you about his murder?"

Jack shook his head. "Years ago, O'Hara and I had the same training officer. Inspector Glen. He was … well, let's just say he was as dirty as they come. Accepted bribes to look the other way when a murder or robbery was committed—or to misplace evidence, or maybe send the name of a key witness to someone who could put that witness out of the way before they could testify. He wasn't above beating a confession out of an innocent man, too, so he'd have someone to pin the blame on. It didn't take O'Hara and me long to discover what he was up to, but what could we do about it? We weren't even official police constables yet, just recruits in training. Who'd take our word above Glen's?"

I studied Jack's face. "I'm guessing you still tried, though?"

Jack released a breath. "Yeah. We tried. We went to the Superintendent and told him what was happening."

"And?"

"And the Superintendent was found dead the next day. Stabbed through the heart. A botched street robbery was the official conclusion."

I swallowed against the cold lump wedged in my throat.

"How did you and O'Hara escape being victims of the same type of unfortunate robberies gone wrong?"

"I'd guess only because the Superintendent didn't name his sources of information. He may not have realised the full extent of what Glen was a part of—just thought he was corrupt but working on his own. That's what O'Hara and I thought, until the Superintendent died. We might have still been in danger—it wouldn't have taken Glen long to work out who'd gone to the Superintendent about him. But then a day or two later, Glen himself was shot in a raid on a criminal's hideout."

"So whatever he knew or suspected died with him." I searched Jack's expression again. "You wouldn't have left it there, though." I didn't have to ask myself what I would have done in Jack's position; I already knew. There were some battles that couldn't be won by a direct assault. But that didn't mean you walked away or stopped fighting. "You and Sergeant O'Hara. You've been investigating quietly ever since, haven't you? Secretly gathering information, assembling evidence."

Under ordinary circumstances, Jack might have grinned and said something about the drawbacks to being married to Sherlock Holmes's daughter. Now he just nodded, his expression equal parts grim and tired. "We never met in person, even off-duty. We didn't want to risk our names being put together. But we'd worked out a system for sending information back and forth. Always in code. We had a couple of places around London where we could leave messages when we had something new to report."

"And it's something to do with those reports of Sergeant O'Hara's that have gone missing now? That's why you wanted his lodgings searched so thoroughly?"

Jack was looking out the hallway window into the street beyond, where carriages were rolling past through the inch or two of wintry slush and mud on the ground. "Yes. I was at O'Hara's lodgings myself just after he died, and I didn't find anything. All the notes he'd kept, the evidence he'd gathered … it was all missing. That doesn't mean the other side's got them. O'Hara could have had another hiding spot—even rented a safe deposit box in a bank somewhere."

"But it also doesn't mean the Syndicate *doesn't* have access to whatever O'Hara knew." And Jack's name was bound to be all over whatever records Sergeant O'Hara had kept.

"You're right."

I said nothing; just looked at him.

Jack turned, meeting my gaze. "You think I should have told you."

There was no point in lying. I knew Jack couldn't always disclose the confidential details of his police work to me, but this was different entirely. To have kept a secret so huge … it felt as though he'd slid a knife between my ribs.

"Yes."

"I wanted to." Jack caught hold of my hand. "I swear I wanted to. But I was afraid. More than afraid. Terrified." He drew a shallow breath. "It's been years. Four years O'Hara and I spent, trying to dig up any kind of evidence to let us fight back. And you know what we've got? Lists of dead witnesses. Lines of investigation that snap as soon as you try to run them down. And now O'Hara's dead."

Jack reached to touch my cheek, and his voice when he went on was both ragged and yet controlled, his eyes dark. "Not much scares me, Lucy. But the thought of what could happen to you if the Syndicate thinks you're any kind of a threat … I'd die if I lost you, Lucy. I'd never leave Becky on her own, but if anything happened to you, everything alive inside me would be gone—killed, too."

He meant it. He meant every word.

I shut my eyes for a second. Tears pricked behind my lids.

I had grown up alone, just as Jack had, wondering what it would be like to have a family of my own. Back then, I would have given anything in the world to know that someday someone would love me this much.

I opened my eyes, drew back, and punched Jack in the shoulder—a solid right hook that made him stagger back a half-step.

"That's what I get for trying to keep all this from you?" he asked, when he'd recovered his balance.

"No. That's what you get for making it very hard to stay angry with you, even though I've every right to."

Finally, Jack gave me a crooked half smile, though it faded almost at once. "I suppose it's no good asking you to stay safely out of this?"

"No." I took his hand and laced my fingers with his. "If you haven't got anywhere on your own in four years, then it's time to see what we both can do."

27. WATSON

Two weeks had elapsed since the explosion of Jerrard's coach and the arrest of the Rexfords. Father and son were still in custody, awaiting trial.

Bail had been denied, given the nature of the purported crimes. The list was impressive indeed: evading arrest, attempted murder of a police officer, attempt to defraud an investment company, actual defrauding of an insurance company, endangerment of the public safety, and the murders of Marcus Thiel, Mr. Jerrard, and his coachman. Those latter three offenses would likely earn father and son the gallows.

Flynn and Becky had been basking in well-deserved praise. The papers and newspaper clippings they had taken from Rexford Hall provided ample hard evidence needed to hold the Rexfords. A search of Jerrard's rooms had also yielded fruit for the prosecution: records of payments to Rexford, and also payments made to a bank in Switzerland. The Queen's Counsel was confident of achieving a guilty verdict, after which both Rexfords would be hanged.

Now, on a snowy Wednesday afternoon, our doorbell rang, and Amy Thiel arrived at our rooms at 221B Baker Street. I took her coat and hung it up. She declined tea. I invited her to take a seat on our sofa. She shook her head.

"Miss Thiel," said Holmes, who had been standing by the mantel. "Please." He gestured towards our sofa.

After a long moment she nodded and sat across from our fireplace, stiffly upright, her blonde hair neatly coiffed, her hands clasped together in her lap.

She drew a breath. "I have come to speak to you about two matters."

Holmes had his attention apparently on refilling his pipe from the Persian slipper, but at that he turned, brows slightly elevated, and took his customary chair to face her. "Please proceed."

She leaned forwards. "First, I have come about the incorporation of the Rexford Works. I have spoken to a group of legitimate underwriters, and they believe the business itself is strong enough to be sustained with Rexford and his son no longer involved. They are willing to proceed with the incorporation, but they would appreciate a short interview with you, simply to assure themselves that your investigation did not uncover any other fatal flaws about the operation."

"They knew of my involvement?" Holmes asked.

"My uncle had told them he would hire you. You were right—he was confident any investor would look favourably on a company investigated by Sherlock Holmes."

"And incorporation would yield far more than the bribe money and the remains of the insurance payments that he had already received," Holmes said. "For such a reward, he was willing to take what he thought was a very small risk."

"He thought his crimes were so clever that even you could not uncover his guilt," I said.

Holmes said, "I shall make myself available for an interview with the underwriters."

Amy relaxed a bit. "That is a relief. Thanks to you, the business will go on," she said, "and four hundred workers will be able to support their families."

Holmes gave one of his fleeting, momentary smiles. "Now, what is the second matter?"

She sat fully upright once more. "Whatever criminal investigation Tobias is involved in—whatever led to his being stabbed. I wish to take part. To help."

"Miss Thiel—" Holmes began.

But Amy interrupted once again. "At least neither you nor Tobias can claim I would be bringing embarrassment to either myself or my family by taking part in a criminal investigation." Her lips twisted. "With both my uncle and my cousin in prison for murder, I should think any damage I do to our family's reputation ought scarcely to register."

"I was not thinking of scandal, Miss Thiel," Holmes said, "But rather the possibility of danger. These are highly unscrupulous people with whom we are dealing. They have already attempted Gregson's murder, and succeeded in many more."

"Please. Give me credit for at least a rudimentary degree of intelligence, Mr. Holmes." Amy's voice was crisp. "I understand there are risks involved. I still wish to offer my services to you in whatever capacity may be most helpful. I cannot bring back my father, but I can help fight against those who tried to kill Tobias."

Holmes considered her a long moment, during which the only sound was the hiss of sleet against the windowpane and the crackle of the coal fire at his back.

"In that case, Miss Thiel," he said at last, "I believe I may have an assignment for you."

THE END

HISTORICAL NOTES

This is a work of fiction, and the authors make no claim that any of the historical locations or historical figures appearing in this story had even the remotest connection with the adventures recounted herein. However ...

1. The explosion at the fictional Rexford Factory at Powder Island was inspired by an incident at the gunpowder factory of Messrs. Curtis and Harvey, in Hounslow. In 1887 an explosion obliterated one of the Hounslow factory buildings while killing the single man who was present at the time. Many of the details of the explosion in this story were taken from the 1887 newspaper account, and from the lengthy Home Office report on the explosion.

2. The Home Office report concluded that, of the many possible causes of the explosion only two, in the judgment of the preparer of the report, were reasonable. "1. The fracture of a portion of the machinery; and 2. Matches maliciously placed upon the platform by some person unknown." As far as the authors are aware, the unknown person was never found, and no arrests were made.

3. The cover image for this adventure is taken from a photograph of the Hounslow Shot Tower, which is the only building from the factory that survives today.

4. The land once occupied by the Hounslow gunpowder factory is now Crane Park Island, a nature preserve managed by the London Wildlife Trust.

5. The massive stone statue of King Henry VIII, erected in 1702, still stands atop the entrance gate of St. Bart's Hospital in London, a brief walk from the Smithfield Market.

6. Corruption in the London Metropolitan Police was a very real problem in the past century. It was vigorously opposed and somewhat eradicated under the watch of Commissioner Edward Bradford, who held many official positions during his distinguished career. Commissioner Bradford appears as a character in many of the Sherlock and Lucy adventures.

7. Lucy James will return.

A NOTE OF THANKS TO OUR READERS

Thank you for reading this Sherlock and Lucy story. We hope you've enjoyed it.

As you probably know, reviews make a big difference! So, we also hope you'll consider going back to the Amazon page where you bought the story and uploading a quick review. You can get to that page by going to this link on our website and scrolling down:

sherlockandlucy.com/project/powder-island
(bit.ly/3avKNSi)

You can also sign up for our mailing list to receive updates on new stories, special discounts, and 'free days' for some of our other books: www.SherlockandLucy.com

About the Authors

Anna Elliott is the author of the *Twilight of Avalon* trilogy, and *The Pride and Prejudice Chronicles*. She was delighted to lend a hand in giving the character of Lucy James her own voice, firstly because she loves Sherlock Holmes as much as her father, Charles Veley, and second because it almost never happens that someone with a dilemma shouts, "Quick, we need an author of historical fiction!" She lives in Pennsylvania with her husband and four children.

Charles Veley is the author of the first two books in this series of fresh Sherlock Holmes adventures. He is thrilled to be contributing Dr. Watson's chapters for the series, and delighted beyond words to be collaborating with Anna Elliott.

Made in the USA
Thornton, CO
04/18/22 20:53:11

52a9c36c-5dbf-4718-b50a-1fe90bbb0092R01